THE MAN WHO WANTED TO BE HAPPY

THE MAN WHO WANTED TO BE HAPPY

LAURENT GOUNELLE

TRANSLATED BY ALAN S. JACKSON

HAY HOUSE

Australia • Canada • Hong Kong • India
South Africa • United Kingdom • United States

First published and distributed in the United Kingdom by:
Hay House UK Ltd, 292B Kensal Rd, London W10 5BE. Tel.: (44) 20 8962 1230;
Fax: (44) 20 8962 1239. www.hayhouse.co.uk

Published and distributed in the United States of America by:
Hay House, Inc., PO Box 5100, Carlsbad, CA 92018-5100. Tel.: (1) 760 431 7695 or
(800) 654 5126; Fax: (1) 760 431 6948 or (800) 650 5115. www.hayhouse.com

Published and distributed in Australia by:
Hay House Australia Ltd, 18/36 Ralph St, Alexandria NSW 2015.
Tel.: (61) 2 9669 4299; Fax: (61) 2 9669 4144. www.hayhouse.com.au

Published and distributed in the Republic of South Africa by:
Hay House SA (Pty), Ltd, PO Box 990, Witkoppen 2068.
Tel./Fax: (27) 11 467 8904. www.hayhouse.co.za

Published and distributed in India by:
Hay House Publishers India, Muskaan Complex, Plot No.3, B-2, Vasant Kunj, New Delhi
– 110 070. Tel.: (91) 11 4176 1620; Fax: (91) 11 4176 1630. www.hayhouse.co.in

Distributed in Canada by:
Raincoast, 9050 Shaughnessy St, Vancouver, BC V6P 6E5. Tel.: (1) 604 323 7100;
Fax: (1) 604 323 2600

A catalogue record for this book is available from the British Library.

ISBN 978-1-84850-857-6

Printed and bound in Great Britain by TJ International, Padstow, Cornwall.

MIX
Paper from
responsible sources
FSC® C013056
www.fsc.org

"WE ARE WHAT WE THINK. . .
WITH OUR THOUGHTS, WE MAKE OUR WORLD."

— BUDDHA

I DIDN'T WANT to leave Bali without meeting him. I don't know why. I wasn't sick; in fact, I've always been in excellent health. I made inquiries about his fees because, with my vacation coming to an end, my wallet was virtually empty. I didn't even dare check my bank account anymore. People who knew him had told me, "You give what you want; you slip it in a little box on a shelf." Right, that calmed me down, even if I was somewhat nervous at the idea of leaving a really small sum for someone who had, it was said, treated the prime minister of Japan.

It was difficult to find his house, which was hidden in a small village a few kilometers from Ubud, in the center of the island. I don't know why, but there are practically no road signs in this country. Reading a map is possible when you have reference points; otherwise, it's as useless as a cell phone in an area without a signal. There remained, of course, the easy solution: ask passersby. Although I'm a man, that's never been a problem. It seems to me that some men feel they are losing their virility if they stoop to that. They prefer to retreat into a silence that means "I know," pretending to get their bearings, until they are completely lost and their wives say, "I told you we should have asked."

The trouble in Bali is that people are so nice that they always say yes. Really. If you say to a girl, "I think you're very pretty," she will look at you with a beautiful smile and reply, "Yes." And when you ask your way, they are so anxious to help that it is unbearable for them to admit that they are unable to. So they point in a certain direction, no doubt randomly.

I was a little on edge when I found myself outside the entrance to the garden.

I don't know why, but I had imagined a fairly luxurious house of the sort you see sometimes in Bali—pools covered with lotus flowers under the kindly shade of frangipani trees displaying great big white blossoms so intoxicatingly perfumed that it's almost indecent. Instead, it was a series of campans, a sort of small house, without any walls, interconnected with each other. Like the garden, they were of great simplicity, quite spare, yet without giving an impression of poverty.

A young woman came to meet me, wrapped in a sarong, her black hair done up in a chignon.

"Hello, what do you want?" she asked me, speaking straightaway in heavily accented English.

My 6'3" frame and blue eyes left little doubt as to my Western origins.

"I've come to see Mr. . . . er . . . Master . . . Samtyang."

"He will come," she told me before disappearing between the bushes and the series of little columns that supported the roofs of the campans.

I remained standing there, slightly stupidly, waiting for His Excellency to deign to come and welcome the humble visitor that I was. After five minutes, which was long enough to make me question why I was here, I saw coming toward me a man of at least 70, perhaps even 80 years of age. The first thing that came to my mind was that I would probably have given him 50 rupiahs if I had seen him begging in the street. I tend to give only to old people: I tell myself that if they are begging at their age, it's because they really don't have a choice. The man walking slowly in my direction was not in rags, granted, but his clothes were disarmingly simple, minimalist, and ageless.

I'm ashamed to admit that my reflex was to think that it was the wrong person. He couldn't be the healer whose reputation had reached overseas. Or else his gift went hand in hand with his lack of good judgment and he charged the prime minister of Japan peanuts. He might also have been a marketing genius, aiming at a clientele of credulous

Westerners avid for a cliché such as the healer living an ascetic life perfectly detached from material things, but accepting a generous remuneration at the end of the session.

He greeted me and welcomed me simply, expressing himself with great gentleness in very good English. The luminosity of his gaze contrasted with the wrinkles in his tanned skin. His right ear was misshapen, as though the lobe had been partly cut off.

He invited me to follow him into the first campan: a roof supported by four small columns, against an old wall, the famous shelf along the wall, a chest in camphor wood and, on the floor, a rush mat. The chest was open and overflowing with documents, among which were plates representing the inside of the human body. These, in another context, would have made me want to scream with laughter, so far were the drawings from present-day medical knowledge.

I took my shoes off before entering the room, as is the tradition in Bali.

The old man asked what was wrong with me, which rudely brought me back to the reason for my visit. What was I looking for exactly, since I wasn't ill? I was about to waste the time of a man whose honesty, not to say integrity, I was beginning to perceive, even if I had as yet no proof of his competence. Did I simply want someone to look into my case, take an interest in me, talk about little old me, and, who knows, discover if there was a way for me to feel better? Perhaps I was obeying a sort of intuition. After all, I had been told he was a great man, which made me curious to meet him.

"I've come for a checkup," I confided, blushing at the idea that this wasn't an annual doctor's exam and my request was out of order.

"Lie down there," he said, pointing to the mat and showing no reaction to the strangeness of my request.

Thus began the first torture session I've experienced in my life—and, I hope, the last. Everything started normally: lying on my back, relaxed, confident, and half amused, I felt him gently palpate different areas of my body. My head, to begin with, then the back of my neck. My arms, all the way down to the last joints of my fingers. Followed by apparently very precise areas on my chest, then my stomach. I was relieved to notice that he passed directly from my stomach to the tops of my legs. My knees, my calves, my heels, the soles of my feet: he touched nearly everything, and it was not particularly unpleasant.

Then, he reached the toes.

I DIDN'T KNOW it was possible to make a man suffer to that extent just by holding the little toe of his left foot between thumb and index finger. I screamed and writhed in every direction on my mat. Seen from afar, it must have looked like a fisherman trying to bait his hook with a 6'3" maggot. I agree that I am a bit of a softy, but what I was experiencing was far more painful than anything I had felt before.

"You are in pain," he said.

No kidding. I stifled a yes between two groans. I no longer even had the strength to shout. He didn't seem affected by my sufferings; he kept a sort of benevolent neutrality. His face even expressed a sort of goodness that was at odds with the treatment he was inflicting on me.

"You are an unhappy person," he said, as if giving his diagnosis.

At that precise moment, yes. Very. I no longer knew whether to laugh or cry at the situation I had put myself in. I may have been doing both at the same time. And to think I could have spent my day on the beach, talking with the fishermen and looking at the pretty Balinese women!

"Your pain in this precise point is the symptom of a more general malaise. If I put the same pressure at the same point on somebody else, he wouldn't feel pain," he said.

Whereupon, he at last let go of my foot, and all at once, I was the happiest of men.

"What do you do?" he asked.

"I am a teacher."

He looked at me for a moment and then walked away, thoughtfully, as if concerned. I felt a little bit as if I'd said something I shouldn't have, or I'd done something stupid. He was looking vaguely in the direction of a bougainvillea in flower a few feet away. He seemed lost in his thoughts. What was I supposed to do? Leave? Cough to remind him of my presence? He extricated me from my confusion by coming back toward me. He sat down on the floor and looked me in the eyes as he spoke.

"What's wrong in your life? Your health is very good. So what is it? Work? Your love life? Your family?"

His questions were direct, and he was looking straight at me, leaving me no way of escape, even though his voice and eyes were kindly. I felt obliged to reply, laying myself bare to a man who was a stranger an hour before.

"I don't know—yes, I could be happier, like everybody, I suppose."

"I'm not asking you to reply for the others, but for you," he calmly replied.

This guy is beginning to annoy me. I do what I want, and it's none of his business, I thought, feeling a mounting anger.

"Let's say I would be happier if I were with someone."

Why did I say that? I felt my anger turning against me. I am really incapable of resisting a question. It's pathetic.

"In that case, why aren't you?"

Right. Now I've got to make a decision, even if that's not my strong point: either I interrupt him and leave, or I play the game to the end.

I heard myself replying: "I wish I were, but for that, some woman would have to be attracted to me."

"What's preventing that?"

"Well, I'm far too thin," I blurted out, red with shame and anger at the same time.

Talking slowly, almost quietly, and making each word stand out, he said, "Your problem is not in your body but in your head."

"No, it's not in my head. It's an objective, concrete fact! You just need to put me on the scales, or measure my pecs or my biceps. You'll see for yourself, and neither the tape measure nor the scales are biased. I can't influence them with my twisted, neurotic mind."

"That's not the question," he replied patiently, keeping his great calm.

"Easily said—"

"Your problem is not your physique, but how you believe women perceive it. Actually, the success that one does or doesn't have with the opposite sex has little to do with physical appearance. Have you never seen people whose looks are a very long way from the standards of beauty but who live with someone rather good-looking?"

"Yes, of course."

"Anyway, most of the people who have your problem have a 'normal' physique, with little defects that they concentrate on. A mouth too narrow, ears too long, a little cellulite, a slight double chin, a nose too big or too small. They think they are a little too short, too tall, too fat, or too thin. When they meet a person who could love them, they have only one obsession: their defect. They are convinced they can't be attractive because of that. And you know what?"

"What?"

"They are right! When you see yourself as ugly, other people see you as ugly. I'm sure women do find you too thin."

"That's right."

"Other people see us as we see ourselves. Who is your favorite actress?"

"Nicole Kidman."

"What do you think of her?"

"An excellent actress, one of the best of her generation. I adore her."

"No, I mean physically."

"Superb, magnificent—she's a bombshell."

"You must have seen *Eyes Wide Shut* by Stanley Kubrick?"

"You watch American films? Have you got a satellite receiver in your campan?"

"If my memory is right, there is a scene where we see Nicole Kidman completely naked, in the company of Tom Cruise."

"Your memory is good."

"Go to the video club in Kuta and have *Eyes Wide Shut* shown. They've got booths for people who don't own a video player. When you get to that scene, freeze the frame and look carefully."

"That shouldn't be too difficult."

"Forget for a few moments that it is Nicole Kidman. Imagine it's someone you don't know and look at her body objectively."

"Yes . . . ?"

"You will observe that she is good-looking; she has a fine body—but not perfect, even so. Her bottom is pretty but could be more rounded, more well formed. Her breasts are not bad, but they could have been bigger, have a prettier curve, and be a little higher, more erect. You will see too that the features of her face are regular, fine, but not of exceptional beauty."

"What are you getting at?"

"There are tens of thousands of women as beautiful as Nicole Kidman. You walk past them in the street every day, and you don't even notice them. Her true force is elsewhere."

"Yes?"

"Nicole Kidman is probably convinced she is superb. She must think that every man desires her and that every woman admires or envies her. She probably sees herself as one of the most beautiful women in the world. She believes it so strongly that other people see her like this."

"In 2006, the British magazine *Eve* voted her one of the five most beautiful women in the world."

"There you are."

"And how do you explain that?"

"That others tend to see us as we see ourselves?"

"Yes."

"Now that you understand this, you're going to do an experiment. For a moment, you are going to imagine something. It doesn't matter whether it's true or not. Just convince yourself that it is true. Are you ready?"

"What? Now? Straightaway?"

"Yes, now. You can close your eyes if it makes it easier for you."

"Okay, I'm ready."

"Imagine that you believe you are very handsome. You are convinced you have a huge impact on women. You're walking on the beach, at Kuta Beach, among all the Australian women on holiday. How do you feel?"

"Really great. Really happy."

"Describe your walk, your posture. Let me remind you that you think you are very handsome."

"My walk . . . how should I describe it? Rather confident but at the same time relaxed."

"Describe your face."

"I'm holding my head up straight; I'm looking in front of me, a slight natural smile on my lips. I am cool and sure of myself at the same time."

"Right. Now imagine how women see you."

"Yes, it's clear; I'm—how shall I put it?—I'm making a certain impact."

"What do they think of your pecs and your biceps?"

"Er . . . they're not really looking at those."

"You can open your eyes. What women find attractive is what emanates from your body, that's all. And that derives directly from the image you have of yourself. When you believe something about yourself, positive or negative, you behave in a way that reflects that thing. You show it to others all the time, and even if it was originally a creation of your mind, it becomes reality for other people, then for you."

"That's possible, even if it's still a little abstract."

"It will become progressively clearer and clearer. I propose to make you discover, through different examples, that practically everything you live has as its origin what you believe."

I was beginning to wonder what I'd walked into. I was a long way then from imagining that our conversation and the exchanges that would follow were going to turn my whole life upside down.

"Imagine," he went on, "that you are convinced you are somebody uninteresting, who bores others when you speak."

"I preferred the other game—"

"This will only last a couple minutes. Imagine it's quite obvious to you: people are bored in your company. Really try to feel what it means to believe that. Are you doing it?"

"Yes. It's awful."

"Remain in that state, keep that in your mind, and now imagine you are having lunch with colleagues or friends. Describe the meal."

"My colleagues are talking a lot. They are talking about their holidays, and I'm not saying very much."

"Stay in that state, but now make an effort and tell them a story about something that happened during your holidays."

"Give me a moment. I'm imagining the scene. All right: it doesn't have much of an effect. They're not really listening to me."

"That's natural. Being convinced you're not interesting, you're going to speak in a way that no one finds riveting."

"Yes."

"For example, since you are unconsciously afraid of boring your colleagues, you will perhaps, without realizing it, speak quickly, garble what you say, so as not to take too much of their time and bore them. As a result, you make no impact, and your story loses all interest. You feel this, and you tell yourself *I'm terrible at telling stories*. Consequently, you get worse and worse and, without fail, one of your colleagues will start speaking again and change the subject. At the end of the meal, everyone will have forgotten that you spoke."

"That's tough."

"When we're convinced of something, it becomes reality, our reality."

I was quite disconcerted by his demonstration.

"Right, okay, but why would anyone be convinced of such a thing?"

"It is probably not your problem, but it is some people's. Everyone believes things about themselves that are special to them. It was just an example.

"To stay with this case, imagine you are convinced of the opposite: you are sure of capturing people's interest, of making an impact on them when you speak. When you start to speak at your lunch with colleagues, you are persuaded that your story will hit the mark. You're going to make them laugh; you'll surprise them or just captivate their attention. Carried along by this conviction, imagine how you speak. Anticipating the expected outcome, you give yourself time to lead up to the subject, to play with your voice. You allow yourself a few well-placed silences to increase the suspense. You know what? They'll be drinking in every word."

"Okay, I understand that what you think becomes reality, but I still have one question."

"Yes?"

"How is it that we begin to believe things about ourselves, positive or negative?"

"Several explanations are possible. First of all, there is what other people say about us. If, for one reason or another, those people are credible in our eyes, then we may believe what they say about us."

"Our parents, for example?"

"Generally it begins, of course, with our parents and the people who bring us up. A young child learns an enormous amount from his or her parents, and, at least up to a certain age, tends to accept everything they say. It's engraved in the child. He or she assimilates it."

"Do you have an example?"

"If parents are convinced their child is beautiful and intelligent, and repeat this constantly, then there is every chance that the child will see herself this way and become very self-confident. That being the case, there won't just be positive effects. Perhaps the child will also be a little arrogant—"

"So it's my parents' fault if I have doubts about my appearance?"

"No, not necessarily. As you will see, there are a number of possible origins for what we believe about ourselves. And, as far as other people's influence is concerned, there aren't just the parents. For example, teachers also sometimes have a great influence."

"That reminds me of something: I was really good in math at school until ninth grade, straight A's. Then in tenth grade, I had a teacher who told us in every class that we were all useless. I remember she used to shout all the time, and you could see the veins in her neck swelling up as she bawled us out. I finished the year with straight F's."

"You probably believed what she was saying."

"Perhaps. But, to be honest, not everyone in the class got straight F's like me."

"They were probably less sensitive than you to the teacher's opinion."

"I don't know."

"An experiment was carried out, in the seventies, by some scientists at an American university. They began by choosing a group of pupils of the same age with the same results in IQ tests: so these children had the same level of intelligence, according to the test. They then divided the group in two. They gave the first subgroup to a teacher who was told, 'Do the same curriculum as usual, but, just to inform you, you should know that these children are more intelligent than average.' The teacher to whom the second group was given was told, 'Do the same curriculum as usual, but, just to inform you, you should know that these children are less intelligent than average.' After a year's worth of classes, the scientists had all the children retake the IQ test. Those in the first subgroup had an average IQ that was distinctly above that of the children in the second group."

"That's crazy."

"It is indeed rather impressive."

"It's incredible! All you have to do is lead a teacher to believe his pupils are intelligent in order for him to make them intelligent; if he's convinced they're stupid, he makes them stupid?!"

"It's a scientific experiment."

"Even so, it's sick to do experiments like that on children."

"Indeed, it is questionable."

"But, by the way, how is it possible? I mean, how can a teacher believing his pupils are idiots result in him making them idiots?"

"There are two possible explanations. First of all, when you talk to someone stupid, how do you express yourself?"

"With super-simple words, very short sentences, and easily understandable ideas."

"There you are. And if you talk like this to children whose brains need stimulating to develop, they will stagnate instead of evolving. That's the first explanation. There's another one, which is more harmful."

"Yes?"

"If you have to deal with a child whom you believe to be stupid, everything about you permanently implies that he is stupid. Not just your vocabulary, as we said a moment ago, but also the way you speak, your facial expressions, your eyes. You're slightly sorry for him or, on the contrary, slightly annoyed, and he notices this. He feels stupid in your presence. And if you're somebody important to him, if your status, your age, and your role mean that you are credible in his eyes, then there is every chance that he will not challenge this feeling. So he will start to believe that he is stupid. You know the rest."

"It's frightening."

"Indeed, it's rather dreadful."

I was very troubled by what I was learning. All these ideas remained as though hanging in the air. We stayed for a few moments without saying anything. A slight wind brought me the subtle scents of the tropical plants that grew freely near the campan. In the distance, a gecko was sounding its characteristic cry.

"There is something that surprises me."

"Yes?"

"I don't want to annoy you, but how do you have access to this sort of information—I mean scientific experiments carried out in the United States?"

"You must allow me to leave certain things a mystery."

I was not going to insist, but I would have liked to know. I found it really hard to imagine an Internet connection in the campan next door. I wasn't even sure the village had a phone line. And, I absolutely could not imagine my healer connecting to scientific forums. I could more readily see him meditating for hours, in the lotus position, in the shade of mangroves.

"You said there were other origins for what we believe about ourselves?"

"Yes, there are the conclusions we draw without realizing it from certain of our life experiences."

"I'd like examples."

"Right, a slightly simplistic example to illustrate

the point: imagine a baby whose parents react only very little to what he does. He cries? His parents don't move. He shouts? Not a word. He laughs? No reaction. You can suppose that there will gradually develop in him the feeling that he has no impact on the world around him, that he can obtain nothing from others. He won't consciously say it to himself, of course, especially at his age. It's just a feeling, a sensation, something in which he is immersed. Now, to simplify the process in the extreme, particularly by supposing that he doesn't have experiences going in the opposite direction, you can imagine that once he becomes an adult, he will become fatalistic, will never go toward others to get what he wants, will not try to change things. If one of his friends sees him at a dead end one day at work, for example, the friend will just have to accept this passivity. There will be no point in trying to convince him to react, to go and knock on doors, to take control of the situation, to contact people—nothing will work. What's more, this friend will perhaps judge him harshly, and yet his attitude is simply the result of the profound conviction, buried deep inside him, that he has no effect on the world around him and can obtain nothing from other people. He won't even be conscious of believing this. For him, that's the way it is; that's reality, his reality."

"Reassure me: parents like that don't exist, do they?"

"It was just an example. Besides, you can imagine the opposite: parents who are very reactive to their child's slightest expression. If he cries, they come running; if he smiles, they are ecstatic. The child will no doubt develop the feeling that he has an impact on his surroundings, and, again cutting a long story short, you can suppose that as an adult he will become someone proactive, or else seductive, who will be convinced of the effect he has on others and will never hesitate to go toward them to get what he wants. But he won't be conscious of what he believes, either. For him, it's just obvious: he has an effect on people. That's the way it is. He doesn't know that a belief has become established in his mind as a result of what he experienced as a child."

The young woman who had welcomed me glided into the campan and left tea and cakes, if that's what you can call that sort of wet, sugary, and sticky paste that you have to eat with your fingers if you respect Balinese tradition. A Balinese proverb says that eating with knife and fork is like making love through an interpreter. You are meant to take the food in your hand, and then slide it into your mouth, pushing it in with your thumb. It takes a little getting used to; otherwise, you'll end up like a baby without a bib.

"So, you begin to believe things about yourself on the basis of what others say to you or what you conclude unconsciously from certain lived experiences. Is that it?"

"Yes."

"And only during childhood?"

"No, let's say it is especially during childhood that most of the beliefs we have about ourselves are formed, but you can also develop them later on, even as an adult. But, in that case, they will generally be the result of very strong emotional experiences."

"For example?"

"Imagine that the first time you speak in public, you make an awful mess of it. You stammer and can't find your words, your voice is stuck in your throat, and your mouth is dry, as if you'd spent three days without drink in the middle of the desert. In the hall, you can hear a pin drop. You can see that people feel sorry for you. Some have a slightly mocking smile. You would give all your savings, and even next year's salary, to be somewhere else and not going through this. You are ashamed just to think back to it. In that case, it's quite possible that you will begin to think you are not made for public speaking. In fact, you have just failed once, that day, in front of those people, talking on that subject. But your brain has generalized the experience by drawing a definitive conclusion from it."

I had finished my cake, and my fingers were now very sticky. I was hesitating between sucking them and wiping them on the mat. Unable to decide, I left my fingers hovering in the air. I was probably developing the belief that I was not made to eat Balinese food.

"When you come back tomorrow, we will discover together other beliefs which are stopping you from being happy," he said to me kindly.

"I didn't know I was coming back tomorrow."

"You don't expect me to believe that your problems are limited to your doubts about your physical appearance? You certainly have other, much more serious problems, and we will tackle them together."

"You're harsh."

"It's not by telling people what they want to hear that you help them change," he replied with a smile.

"You know, I thought you were a healer, that you only concerned yourself with illnesses and pains."

"In the West, you are used to separating the body and the mind. Here, we think the two are closely linked and form a coherent whole. Perhaps we'll have the opportunity to talk more about this."

"Just one final question. I am more comfortable if these things are clear, even if it embarrasses me to talk about them: how much will I owe you for your help, for the time you give me?"

He looked at me closely, then said, "I know your profession leads you, too, to transmit things to others. It's enough for me if you undertake not to keep what you discover to yourself."

"You have my word."

As I left, I nonetheless slipped a bill into the little box on the shelf.

"It's for your work on my toes."

THE ROAD TO Ubud is particularly beautiful. I hadn't noticed this on the journey there, preoccupied as I was by the worry of finding my way. Twisting and twining in places it goes through little fields edged with wild banana trees and crossed here and there by a stream. This hilly region in the center of the island is subject to the constant alternation of sun and rain, a warm rain that intensifies the smells of nature. The climate favors the explosion of lush tropical vegetation.

Around a corner, I saw three Balinese men at the edge of a field, a few yards from the road. They must have been between 20 and 30, slender, and . . . entirely naked. I was most surprised by their unexpected appearance. I was not aware of an absence of modesty in Balinese culture. Had they just been for a swim after a day of laboring in the fields? They were walking peacefully side by side. Our eyes met as I arrived next to them. I didn't manage to interpret the strange looks they gave me. Were they embarrassed to encounter me on this lonely road? Had they noticed my surprise at their nakedness?

The road continued and, as Ubud drew near, went through small villages. The houses betrayed a certain poverty, and yet the streets were always well cared for, clean, and full of flowers. On the ground before each door were offerings of flowers and food placed on interwoven pieces of banana leaves. These offerings were renewed regularly throughout the day.

The Balinese live in the sacred. Their religion does not depend on codified rites at fixed times or certain days of the week. No, they are in direct contact with the gods. They seem imbued with their faith, permanently inhabited by it. Always calm, gentle, and smiling, they are no doubt, along with the Mauritians, the nicest people on Earth. You get the impression that nothing can upset these even-tempered people. They greet everything that comes their way with the same serenity.

Without fail, Bali makes visitors think of paradise, and yet they would no doubt be surprised to learn that the word *paradise* does not exist in Balinese. It is the natural element of the Balinese, who no more have a word to refer to it than fish have one to refer to the water that surrounds them.

I was thinking back to my meeting with the

healer, and I still felt under the spell of our conversation. The man had a special aura. I was excited by what he had revealed to me, even if what he said had sometimes been disconcerting. I had never imagined that I would one day find myself on the other side of the world, listening to an old Balinese sage's commentary on Nicole Kidman's breasts and bottom.

At the exit from Ubud, I forked off to the east to go back home. The day had been rich in emotions, and I felt the need to be on my own for a while to allow all I had discovered to settle in me. It would take me more than an hour to reach the little fishing village on the east coast where I had rented a bungalow on the edge of a remote, pretty beach of gray sand. Fortunately, the tourists preferred the expanses of white sand in the south of the island, so it was rare to come across them on "my" beach. Only a Dutch couple had taken up residence in a slightly isolated spot. They were not unpleasant, and I seldom met them. My bungalow belonged to a family who lived farther inland. I had rented it for a month at a rate very acceptable to me, very profitable for them: I like situations where everyone is a winner. The beach remained deserted in the morning; some village children would come to play in the afternoon. The only other comings and goings were those of the fishermen, whom I sometimes heard setting out to sea in their pirogues at five in the morning. I had gone with them once, even though, since I don't speak Balinese, it had been difficult to make them understand and therefore to get their agreement.

It remained one of my happiest memories of Bali. We had set out before dawn, and I had not felt too confident in the unstable pirogue. It sat at water level, and I could see virtually nothing in the black of the moonless night. But the fishermen knew their craft, and that day I experienced what confidence was—blind confidence, as it happened. The lapping of the water and the cool breeze brushing my face were almost the only elements that my roused senses could pick up. Three-quarters of an hour later, I saw the sun slowly appear on the horizon, like a floodlight lighting a scene at ground level, all at once bringing into existence the grandiose scenery. It was immense, magical. I discovered at the same time the enormity of the sea, the gigantic scale of the sky, and the minuteness of the pirogue, which seemed to be floating by magic on a bottomless abyss, like a match dropped on the ocean. I also discovered the smiles of the fishermen and suddenly felt happy without knowing why.

On the way back, we had seen some dolphins near the pirogue, and I expressed the desire to dive with them, with the idiotic reflex of a Westerner who has been to too many theme parks. The Balinese had stopped me, getting me to understand as best they could that dolphins swimming on the surface might be followed down below by sharks hunting the same shoal of fish. Their case was strong enough to convince me, and I contented myself with admiring these beauties of nature, free in their movements, free to go where they will, free to live their lives.

I stopped by the road to eat a nasi goreng at a stall, a typical dish based on rice, like nearly all Balinese cooking. After four weeks, just seeing rice was almost enough to take away my appetite. I arrived at my bungalow at nightfall, an ideal moment to go and walk on the beach without meeting a soul. I took off my shoes and set off straightaway. As foreseen, the beach was deserted, and I walked for a long time along the water's edge, my trousers rolled up.

Quickly, my wandering thoughts turned to my encounter with the healer, and I thought about all he had revealed to me. So we humans had developed beliefs about ourselves as a result of the influence of the people around us or conclusions drawn unconsciously from our experiences. I was willing to accept that, but how far did these beliefs go? We had seen that you could believe yourself to be good-looking or ugly, intelligent or stupid, interesting or boring. You could believe in your ability to influence things or, on the contrary, believe that you're incapable of obtaining anything from others. In what other areas could you develop these beliefs? I understood that you could believe in a certain number of things and that these beliefs would then have an influence on your life. But how much? I wondered in what way my own beliefs had influenced the course of my life and in what way, as a result of chance encounters and experiences, I could have believed other things that would then have given a different direction to my life.

The only answer to my questionings was the murmuring of the water under my feet, splashing the silence of the deserted beach. The palm trees at its edge were perfectly still; no wind blew in their delicate branches. I had gotten into the habit of taking a swim every evening. I took off my trousers and T-shirt and slipped into the warm water. I swam for a long time without thinking about anything, under the benevolent gaze of the young moon.

I AWOKE AFTER a particularly deep sleep and discovered that the sun was already high in the sky. I ate some fruit for breakfast and went for a morning walk in the little wood that extends behind the beach. As I arrived near the bungalow of Hans and Claudia, the Dutch couple, I recognized their voices.

"Isn't lunch ready yet?" asked Hans. He was sitting on a small rock, a book on his knees.

He had dark gray hair, an inexpressive face, and rather thin lips.

"Soon, darling, soon."

Claudia, a nice, gentle woman, 40ish, her round face framed by pretty, blonde curls, was cooking skewers of fish on a barbecue.

"You're using too much charcoal. There's no point; they're ruined."

He said that without realizing it was a reproach. For him, it was a fact, that was all.

"But otherwise it cooks too slowly," she explained.

The last time I saw them, Claudia was cleaning the bungalow while Hans was reading his wretched book. I wondered what could bring a woman to take on the role of the housewife in the 21st century. Hans wasn't macho in the normal sense. For him, it was probably just "normal" for his wife to take care of that. The question had no doubt never even been debated.

"Hey, Julian. How nice to see you!" Claudia said when she noticed me.

"Good morning, Julian," said Hans.

"Good morning."

"Would you like to share our fish with us?" she offered.

Almost imperceptibly, Hans raised an eyebrow.

"No thanks. I've just had my breakfast."

"You've only just got up?" asked Hans. "We've already done two visits this morning: the temple of Tanah Lot and the Subak Museum, in Tabanan."

"That's great—congratulations."

He didn't hear the irony in my reply. Hans was one of those people who listens to words, but decodes neither the tone of voice nor the facial expressions of the speaker.

"You don't do much sightseeing, I get the impression. Doesn't it interest you?"

"It does, but I especially like to feel atmospheres, walk in the villages, talk with people, try to put myself in their place. You know, understand their culture."

"Julian likes to discover culture from inside; but you, darling, prefer to understand culture in books," said Claudia.

"Yes, it's faster. You save time," said Hans, out-doing his wife.

I agreed. What was the point of arguing?

"Would you like to come with us this evening?" asked Claudia. "We're going to a gamelan concert in Ubud, then, at nightfall, we'll go and watch the turtles on Pemuteran beach. It's the period when their eggs hatch. It lasts one or two nights, at the most. After that, it'll be too late."

The prospect of an evening with Hans didn't thrill me, but I really wanted to see the baby turtles. And I could tell it would particularly please Claudia if I accepted.

"Okay, it's nice of you to offer. I'll already be in the Ubud area this afternoon, so I'll meet you there. Give me the address."

"It's in the village hall, you know, next to the big market. At seven o'clock," said Claudia.

"You're visiting the galleries?" asked Hans.

Ubud was the artists' village, and there was an abundance of art galleries.

"No, I'm going to see—how shall I put it?—a sort of spiritual master."

"Oh, really, what for?"

I knew his question was sincere. Hans was the

sort to ask you why you were going to the cinema, to church, or to the cemetery, or why you no longer wore a pair of trousers that were terribly out of fashion but still had some wear in them. Anything that didn't stem from a rational process (rational for him) was a freak of nature.

"He's helping me become aware of certain things. And, in a way, he's also helping me to find myself again."

"Find yourself again?"

The tone of his voice was both amused and taken aback.

"Yes, sort of."

"But, if you're lost, what proof is there you'll find yourself again in Ubud rather than in New York or Amsterdam?"

Very funny. There really are people who are completely impervious to the spiritual dimension of life.

"I'm not lost. If you open a dictionary—by the way, you ought to enjoy reading it, the emotional level is just right for you—you will see that there are several meanings for the verb *find*. As it happens, 'to find oneself again' means to know oneself better in order to have a life more in harmony with what one is."

"Don't get angry, Julian."

"I'm not angry," I lied.

"Darling, leave Julian alone," said Claudia. "By the way, do you still go diving?"

"Yes, nearly every day."

"We went diving the first day," said Hans. "We were lucky: the weather was fine and the water clear. In one hour, we saw the essentials of what there was to see."

"I return often; I get great pleasure from diving among the fish, getting close to them. They are so tame that you can almost touch them."

I was expecting him to ask me what for.

"Man is descended from fish. Julian is reconnecting with his rediscovered origins."

"And you're about to eat one of your ancestors' descendants grilled on the barbecue. There's a fine thing. Anyhow, I'll leave you to your lunch—bon appétit! See you this evening."

"Happy hunting. And don't lose hope: there's still the lost property office in Jakarta!"

"See you this evening," said Claudia.

I resumed my walk, thinking about Hans. I wondered what his "problem" might be. He was a bit weird. All the same, I felt he wasn't nasty; he didn't want to hurt me. He was just impervious to certain things.

I returned to my bungalow, quickly got ready, then leapt into my car. The route seemed simpler this time, and I arrived outside Master Samtyang's house in the middle of the afternoon.

THE SAME YOUNG woman greeted me pleasantly and led me directly to the campan I had been in the day before. This time I was able to observe the place more calmly. It was both spare and beautiful. It radiated great serenity, peace, and harmony, and I was beginning to really like it. Such a spot allowed you to let go of a number of things. Here, you left many of your worries at the entrance. Time was suspended. I had the impression I could have spent years here without getting a single wrinkle.

I didn't see him come. I turned around, and he was behind me. We greeted each other, and he informed me that at this time of day he would not be able to give me much time. Pity.

"So, you went to the video club in Kuta?" he asked me.

"Er . . . no," I admitted slightly pathetically.

He said, without the slightest trace of reproach

or authority, "If you really want me to accompany you on the path that will take you forward in your life, it is necessary that you do what I ask. If you make do with relying on me and listening to me, not much will happen. Are you ready for an undertaking of that sort?"

"Yes."

Did I really have a choice, since I wanted to continue our relationship?

"Tell me: why didn't you go to Kuta?"

"Er . . . actually, I was a bit tired last night, and I needed to rest."

In a kindly voice, he said, "Even if you lie to others, at least don't lie to yourself."

"Excuse me?" I was taken aback.

"What were you afraid of?"

His voice radiated gentleness, and his eyes looked deep into mine. To my innermost self. And yet, I felt no intrusion. It was just that I felt seen. This man was reading me like an open book.

"What could you have lost by going there?"

How did he know how to ask *the* question, to delicately place his finger exactly where it was needed?

After a certain silence, I heard myself reply, "I think I wanted to keep intact my admiration for my favorite actress."

"You were afraid to lose your illusions."

It was strange, but it was true. All the stranger that, the day before, I had known that he was right about her. So why refuse the truth?

"Perhaps," I said.

"It's natural. Human beings are very attached to all the things they believe. They don't go looking for the truth. They just want a certain form of equilibrium, and they manage to build a more or less coherent world for themselves on the basis of their beliefs. It reassures them, and unconsciously they cling to it."

"But why don't we realize that what we believe is not reality?"

"Remember that what we believe becomes reality."

"I'm not sure I'm following you entirely, you know. Perhaps it's a bit too philosophical for me. Despite being a dreamer, I am still rational. For me, reality is reality."

"It's very straightforward, in fact. If I asked you to close your eyes, to cover your ears, and to describe in detail all that is around you, you would not be able to describe everything. It's natural; the scene comprises billions of pieces of information, and you haven't picked them all up. You have only perceived part of reality."

"In other words?"

"For example, on the visual level, there are numerous pieces of information—the layout of the walls and the pillars of the different campans that can be seen; the trees, bushes, and plants with thousands of leaves that move about in a certain way in the breeze. To this are added furniture, objects, drawings. Each of these objects is made of different materials. These materials are not all the same; the colors are not the same. There is also a mass of information concerning the light, the shadows, the sky, the clouds, the sun. Just my body, on its own, is sending you thousands of pieces of information relative to my posture, my movements, my eyes, the expressions on my face, which are changing from one second to the next. And all that is just the visual information!

"To this you must add auditory information: the different noises, close or far, the multiple modulations of my voice, its volume, its tonality, the rhythm of my words, the sound of our clothes when we move, the insects buzzing, the birds calling in the distance, the rustle of the leaves in the wind, and so on.

"But that is not all, either. You are also flooded with information about smells and sensations: the temperature of the air, its humidity, the scents of the different plants that surround us, scents that change according to the movement of the air, the feeling of the many points of contact between your body and the ground, the—"

"Okay, okay, you've convinced me," I interrupted. "I admit I wouldn't have been capable of transmitting all those pieces of information with my eyes closed and my ears covered. It's true."

"And that is for a very good reason: you are not conscious of all these pieces of information. There are too many, and your mind unconsciously sorts them. Some you pick up, others not."

"Yes, no doubt."

"What is really interesting is that this sorting process is not the same for you and for me. If we asked several people to do this exercise and list what they observed of their environment, we wouldn't get two lists that were the same. Each person would do his or her own particular sorting."

"Right."

"And the sorting isn't done randomly."

"What do you mean?"

"The sorting process is specific to each person, and it depends especially on beliefs—on what that person believes about the world in general, in short, on his or her vision of life."

"Yes?"

"Our beliefs will result in us filtering reality, that is to say, filtering what we see, hear, and feel."

"That is still a little abstract for me."

"I am going to give you an example, a slightly oversimplified example."

"Okay."

"Imagine that you are unconsciously convinced that the world is dangerous, that you must be wary of it, that you must protect yourself. That is your belief, all right?"

"Yes."

"If this belief is inscribed in you, then, in your opinion, what is your attention going to fix itself on in the present moment? What information are you going to pick up if you believe, deep down, that the world is dangerous?"

"Well. Let's see . . . I don't know. I imagine I would start by being a little wary of you, since, after all, I don't know you! I think I would observe your face, especially, in order to try and read your thoughts, to understand what lies behind your kind words. And I would try to spot any inconsistencies in what you say, to know if you are reliable or not. And then I'd keep an eye on the garden gate to make sure it stayed open and I could leave easily if there were a problem. What else? Let's see . . . perhaps I'd pay attention to that beam, which seems to stay in place only by a miracle and which might fall on me. And I'd keep an eye on the gecko that I can hear walking between the beams, because I'd be afraid he'd come down and bite me. I would notice too that the mat is worn out and I might pick up splinters if I didn't watch out. There you are."

"That's it. Your attention will be caught by the potential risks which exist in every situation, and if you were asked to describe the situation, eyes closed, those are the factors that would come to your mind."

"Probably."

"Now imagine that you had the opposite belief, that the world is friendly, that people are nice, honest, and trustworthy, and that life offers numerous pleasures that are yours for the taking. Behave as if that conviction were deep inside you. What would your attention be turned to, at this moment, and what could you describe with your eyes shut and your ears blocked?"

"I think I would talk about the plants, which are really very beautiful, about this pleasant breeze, which is making the heat bearable. I think I would talk about the gecko, too, because I would have said to myself, *There's a gecko in the roof. That's cool—there won't be any insects crawling around!* And then I would describe the serene face of this friendly man who is revealing all sorts of interesting things to me without even charging!"

"Exactly! What we believe about reality, about the world around us, acts like a filter, like a selective pair of glasses, which leads us to see the details that go along with what we believe—to such an extent that it reinforces our beliefs. We've come full circle.

"If you think that the world is dangerous, you will pay attention to all the real or potential dangers, and you will increasingly have the impression of living in a dangerous world."

"It's logical, after all."

"But it doesn't stop there. Our beliefs will also allow us to *interpret* reality."

"Interpret?"

"A moment ago, you mentioned the expression on my face. That expression, just like my gestures, can be interpreted in different ways. Your beliefs will help you find an interpretation: a smile will be perceived as a sign of friendship, kindness, and seduction, or irony, mockery, and condescension. An insistent gaze might be a sign of strong interest or, on the contrary, a threat, a desire to destabilize.

And each person will be convinced of his interpretation. What you believe about the world leads you to give a meaning to all that is ambiguous or uncertain, and that reinforces your beliefs. Once again."

"I'm beginning to understand why you said that what we believe becomes our reality."

"Yes, but it doesn't stop there."

"Wow, this is killing me!"

"When you believe something, it leads you to adopt certain behaviors that will have an effect on the behavior of others in a way that will, once again, reinforce what you believe."

"Hey, now you're getting complicated."

"It's simple. Let's stay with the same example: you are convinced that the world is dangerous, that you have to be wary. How are you going to behave when you meet new people?"

"I'm going to remain on my guard."

"Yes, and your expression will probably be fairly opaque, not very inviting."

"No doubt."

"But these people who are meeting you for the first time are going to see it, feel it. How are they themselves going to behave toward you?"

"There is a good chance that they will remain on their guard and not open up to me."

"Exactly! Except that you are going to see that; you are going to feel that they are aloof, slightly strange with you. Guess how you are going to interpret it, swayed by your beliefs."

"Obviously, I'm going to tell myself that I'm right to be suspicious."

"Your beliefs will be reinforced."

"That's awful."

"In this case, it is. But it also works in the opposite way: if you are, deep down, convinced that everyone is friendly, you are going to behave very openly with people. You will smile, be relaxed. And that, of course, is going to lead them to open up, to relax in your company. You will unconsciously have the proof that the world is indeed friendly. Your belief will be reinforced. But you must understand that this process is unconscious. That is why it is powerful. At no moment will you consciously say to yourself, *It's just what I thought—people are friendly.* No. You won't need to say it because, for you, it's normal. That's the way it is: people are friendly, it's obvious. In the same way, those who think that they must at all costs be wary of others find it normal to meet aloof, even unpleasant people, even if they actually hate feeling this way."

"It's crazy. In the end, without realizing it, we each create our own reality, which is in fact nothing but the fruit of our beliefs. Incredible!"

"That last word is well chosen."

I sensed a certain satisfaction in him. He must have been seeing that I was beginning to understand the force and the extent of the theory. I was truly astounded. I now saw that human beings were victims of their own ideas, their own convictions, their own "beliefs," to use his word. The most awful thing, perhaps, was that they didn't know it. And for a good reason: they didn't even realize they believed what they believed. Their beliefs were not conscious. I wanted to shout it out to the whole world, to explain that they were ruining their lives because of things that were not even real. I saw myself driving around the planet in one of those vans used for advertisements. I would shout into the loudspeaker and broadcast my amplified voice from town to town: "Ladies and gentlemen, you absolutely must stop believing what you believe. You are making yourselves suffer." It would only take three days for the men in white coats to come and put me in a straightjacket.

"Right, just one thing, though: these beliefs we have, what areas do they concern? How far do they go?"

"We have all developed beliefs about ourselves, about others, about our relationships with others, about the world that surrounds us, about everything, more or less. Each one of us carries within himself a constellation of beliefs. They are numberless and direct our lives."

"And some are positive, and some are negative, right?"

"No, not exactly. We can't judge our beliefs. The only thing that can be stated is that they are not reality. What is more interesting, however, is to understand their effects. Each belief tends to produce both beneficial effects and limiting effects.

Now, I recognize that certain beliefs lead to more beneficial effects than others."

"Yes, it seems to me that it is in our interest to believe that the world is friendly, isn't it? What's more, I can't see how the belief that the world is dangerous can have beneficial effects."

"It does, though. Such a belief would lead you, of course, to protect yourself to excess, you would no doubt spoil your life a little, but the fact is that, if one day you met a real danger, you would perhaps be more protected than someone who believes that everything is for the best."

"Mmm."

"That's why it is important to become aware of what we believe, then to realize that they are only beliefs and, finally, discover their effects on our lives. It can help us understand many of the things we live through."

"By the way, yesterday you said that we would touch on what it is that is preventing me from being happy."

"Yes, but first I am going to give you work to do on your own: I have two tasks, which you must carry out after our session, before we see each other again."

"Right."

"The first consists of dreaming while staying awake."

"That I think I can do."

"You will dream that you are in a world where everything is possible. Imagine there is no limit to what you are capable of achieving. Act as if you had every qualification in the world, all the qualities that exist, a perfect intelligence, highly developed interpersonal skills, a wonderful body—everything you want. Everything is possible."

"I sense I'm going to like this dream."

"Imagine what your life looks like in this setting: what you do, your job, your leisure, how your life unfolds. Keep at the forefront of your mind that everything is possible. Then write it down and bring it to me."

"Fine."

"Your second task involves doing certain investigations."

"Investigations?"

"Yes, I want you to gather the results of scientific research carried out in the United States on the effects of placebos. We will then talk together."

"But where am I going to find that?"

"In the United States, all the pharmaceutical laboratories carry out research because they have to; they are not allowed to put a drug on the market if it hasn't been scientifically proven to be more effective than a placebo, that is, an inactive substance. Indirectly, that provides precise statistics on the effectiveness . . . of placebos. Nobody uses these statistics. But I find them worthy of interest. I know that laboratories have produced certain results. You'll find them."

"You know them?"

"Of course."

"Well, in that case, why are you asking me to find them? We would save a lot of time by talking about them straightaway. You know, I am flying back home on Saturday; that leaves few opportunities for us to meet—"

"Because listening to someone giving you a piece of information and finding it for oneself at the source is not at all the same thing."

"Forgive me, but I don't see what that changes."

"If I talk to you about them, you can always doubt the figures that I give you. And, knowing you slightly, I know you will not fail to do that! Perhaps not at the moment, but later. Besides, it's not by listening to someone talking that you make progress. It's by doing, having experiences."

"But where will I be able to get this information? I'm not in a hotel. I have no way of getting access to the Internet, and I have never seen an Internet café on the island."

"He who allows himself to be halted by the first difficulty in his path does not go far in life. Come on. I have confidence in you."

"One last thing: when can I come tomorrow to find you completely available, with more time?"

He looked at me for a few moments smilingly. I wondered if I had said something I shouldn't again.

"First and foremost, do not start thinking that you need me. The time I can give at the time you come will be sufficient."

8

GOING BACK TO my car, I wondered how this man could remain so calm, serene, with such a kindly look, while sometimes saying things that absolutely weren't what I wanted to hear.

He was really unusual, and I continued to be amazed by his knowledge of Western news. I would have sworn he'd never left his village, so I found it hard to understand how this old man from the other side of the world drew his wisdom from Western research. Weird.

I was beginning to know the road, and I was in Ubud in no time. The sun set early, and it was already dark when I parked near the great market. The scent of incense was coming from the garden terrace of a small restaurant. The Balinese often use incense to repel mosquitoes. You could see sticks burning on saucers laid out in gardens or at the entrance to houses. It contributed to the intoxicating nighttime atmosphere in Ubud.

I slipped into the restaurant, sat beneath a tree, and ordered grilled fish. There were candles on the tables in the garden, to which were added torches stuck in the grass, burning slowly, giving off a soft, warm light. Shouts could be heard here and there, coming from the street—no doubt Balinese calling to passing foreigners to offer services as unofficial taxi drivers. I had an hour to pass before the concert. Bali was the only place in the world where I didn't look at my watch every half hour. Here, time had no importance. It was the time that it was, and that was that. Like the weather, no one tried to figure out what it would be like. In any case, every day would have sun and rain. That's the way it was. The Balinese accepted what the gods gave them without asking embarrassing questions.

I thought again of the wise man's request that I dream of an ideal life where I would be happy. I needed a little time to get myself into the shoes of someone allowed to do anything and imagine what my life would be like. You don't have those sorts of thoughts every day. Personally, I was more used to noting each day everything that wasn't right in my life, rather than thinking about what I would really like it to be . . .

When I allowed myself to dream, the first thing that came to mind was that, if everything was possible, I would change my job. Teaching was, certainly, a noble and rewarding profession, but I had had enough of teaching a subject to children who didn't like it and were even profoundly bored by it. I knew, of course, that by setting about it differently, you could increase their motivation and learn to interest them, but I was obliged to apply to the letter the official syllabus and stick to current teaching methods, methods completely unsuited to today's students. I couldn't bear being caught between the totally different demands of the administration and the classroom anymore. I wanted fresh air, a total job change, to fulfill myself in an artistic field. I dreamed of making my passion my profession, and my passion was photography. I especially loved capturing facial expressions with portraits that revealed a subject's personality, his emotions, his moods. Even wedding photography attracted me. If anything was possible, I would start my own photography studio. Not one of those factories for churning out dull, posed photos—no, a studio specializing in candid photos that captured the attitudes and personalities of my subjects. My photos would tell stories. Looking at them, you would understand what each person thinks and feels. They would decode the emotions of the parents, the hopes or the fears of the in-laws, the look in the eyes of the elder sister who is wondering when her turn will come, or the divorcees telling each other that these newlyweds believe in Santa Claus. I would want to immortalize people's happiness, also, so that all their lives, with a single glance, they could plug back into the atmosphere and emotions of the big day. A successful photo says so much more than a long speech.

My studio would have a lot of success and would become famous. Magazines would publish some of my photos. I would at last be recognized for my talent. Yep, it'd be cool. I would hold my prices down to allow a broad public to buy my services. Even so, I'd manage with no trouble to double or even triple the amount I'd earned as a teacher. I could at last buy a house. A lovely house I'd design and have built. I would have a garden, and I'd read books there on the weekends, stretched out in a deck chair, in the shade of a lime tree. I would lie in the grass and have a siesta, my nostrils tickled by the scent of the daisies. And then, of course, I'd be with a woman I loved and who loved me. That went without saying. I would also learn to play the piano. I'd always wanted to play an instrument! This time, I'd do it. And then I'd play Chopin nocturnes in the evening, in my grand drawing room, with the fire crackling in the hearth. Every now and then, I'd have friends over and play for them. My happiness would be contagious.

"Your fish, sir."

"Er, sorry?"

"Would you like lemon or spicy sauce?"

"Lemon, please."

The fish was presented whole on my plate, and I

had the impression its eye was looking at me. I started to feel guilty about dreaming of happiness while this fish had died for me. He was reminding me of this by staring at me.

I was almost surprised to observe that my dream was not enormous. I didn't need to become a millionaire to be happy, nor to be a rock star or a well-known politician. And yet, this simple dream and the happiness it contained seemed inaccessible. I was almost annoyed with the healer for having half opened a door onto what my life could have been. A door which, once closed again, left a bitter taste. It made obvious to my consciousness the immense gap between dream and reality.

There remained the other task he had given me. I wondered where I could find Internet access. No doubt in a hotel, as long as it was sufficiently luxurious to be well equipped. But there was a risk I'd be refused access because I wasn't a guest. Right, I'd do it tomorrow. I'd test my luck in one of the palaces on the coast. I'd invent some fib and try to find a way.

The fish didn't look as though it approved of my idea. It went on staring at me with its guilt-provoking eye. My appetite gone, in the end I asked for the bill, leaving my plate half full. Sorry, old chap—you died in vain.

Outside, I found again the relaxed atmosphere of the street. I came across Hans and Claudia outside the concert hall. Standing up, they were hurriedly eating a sort of unappetizing sandwich. Naturally:

why seek enjoyment? You waste less time eating a snack, and it's cheaper. In short, more rational!

"Good evening, Julian!" they said in chorus.

"Good evening to the pair of you! Right, how many temples did you visit this afternoon?"

"Let's say we used our day most profitably," replied Hans.

"The concert's about to start," announced Claudia.

The concert hall was, in fact, a sort of open-air amphitheater. It was already almost full, and we sat at the back, right at the top, but facing the stage. As a demanding music lover, I had a few ideas about gamelan—a sort of large bamboo xylophone that produced a limited range of crude sounds. That evening, there were no less than eight on the stage, and, when the concert began, I was surprised by the volume of noise that rose up in the amphitheater. At first the sound seemed deafening, even cacophonic, but a sort of overall coherence appeared to me later. I soon had to recognize there was something enchanting in this music that lacked harmony to Western ears. After a while, the repetitiveness of the melodies hypnotized me, I found myself in a sort of trance, as if borne along by the obsessive sounds that had a hold on my brain. A strong smell of incense was spreading in the amphitheater, in different places, and was circling round the audience. Ten or twenty minutes had gone by, perhaps more because I was losing my sense of time, when

the dancers appeared on stage, dressed in their sublime, richly colored, refined traditional dress. Their
hair was done in sophisticated chignons decorated
with pearls and fine ribbons. Their dance steps were
precise, delicate, each movement demonstrating incredible femininity and grace. At a distance, I could
see their upturned eyes, and, all of a sudden, I understood that they were in a trance; they were dancing
in a hypnotic state. It was impressive to watch them
moving perfectly in rhythm to the sound of the
gamelans, which sustained their trance and com-
municated it to the spectators. Their movements
on stage were measured, their coordination perfect.
Their hands played a crucial role in the dance. They
moved in a series of delicate gestures, very codified,
as elegant as they were precise. The public was cap-
tivated, and I could feel it vibrate in harmony with
the dancers. The aroma of the incense bewitched us.
Only Hans looked at his watch from time to time.
Claudia was enthralled by the spectacle. I had the
impression she was going to levitate, a phenomenon
that would have greatly interested her scientist husband. The rhythm got progressively faster, and the
mind-numbing sound of the gamelan grew louder,
taking control of my brain and possessing my soul,
which was no longer quite my own. The perfume
of the incense occupied my body and impregnated
each fiber of my being. The stage lights swirled in
my head while each cell of my body vibrated to the
rhythm of the percussion instruments.

I FOUND IT difficult to drive at night after such a concert. Fortunately, all I had to do was follow Hans and Claudia's car. I knew I could trust Hans: he had not been affected by the performance. I was driving on autopilot, and yet the road seemed very long. We went through woods, fields, and innumerable villages where I had to concentrate so as not to hit the few people still present in the streets. The hardest was to avoid the cars that were driving in all directions, most of the time without lights. The Balinese believe in reincarnation and, as a result, are not afraid of death. It makes them very reckless, whether they are pedestrians or drivers. The poor mortal that I am had to be extra vigilant.

It was nearly midnight when we arrived on the beach at Pemuteran. The sky was black, but points of light indicated the presence of several people at different places on the beach. The moon occasionally came out from the clouds that were trying to hold it back, casting bright, cold light on the little waves licking the sand. The three of us were stopped by an official who was controlling access to the beach.

"Good evening. We've come to see the turtles," said Hans.

"Good evening. You may go onto the beach if you respect the rules: you must stay at least six feet away from the adult turtles. You must not raise your voice. And you must stay on the land side of the turtles: you aren't allowed to walk in the area that separates them from the sea."

"Right."

"Have a good evening."

We crossed the sand in silence, breathing in the warm night air heavy with subtle sea scents. We could make out large dark masses spread out across the beach: turtles, each more than a yard long and weighing about 250 pounds. They were immobile, as if asleep on the sand. The pallid light that appeared periodically, like some celestial lighthouse, made them look like disturbing prehistoric creatures. We gazed at them, speechless, for a long while. Nothing could have made us disturb their tranquillity. They were preparing to accomplish the most beautiful act in the world in a religious silence, barely ruffled by the infinitesimal lapping of the waves. We were plunged into a universe of slowness, immersed in calm, numbed by our fascination for this rare moment, feeling the muffled pulsations of our hearts resonating deep inside us.

Long minutes went by like this, none of us saying a word; then we headed for a group of people gathered a little farther on. They belonged to an association for the protection of nature, sent here for the occasion. They were watching the eggs until they hatched, because, once they were laid, they were abandoned in the sand by their mothers. They explained that they kept a register of annual births to follow the statistics from year to year. The turtles had been hunted for centuries, but the government, alerted to the growing threat of the species' disappearance, had finally prohibited all trade in them. Since then, poaching had taken off, and the officials were doing what they could to watch the few beaches concerned during the short laying season: one or two nights a year.

The mothers themselves had been born here, on this same beach, more than 50 years ago. They had been traveling all those years, had covered tens of thousands of miles, and had come back to give life at the exact spot where they had been born half a century before. No one knew why; no scientist could explain it. That's the way it was. And it was very moving.

These silent turtles were guardians of an age-old secret, bearers of an unknown wisdom. Why did they come back here? How had they managed to navigate across the oceans to come precisely to this spot, to the site of their birth? What was the meaning of it? So many questions would remain unanswered.

We waited for nearly three hours for the eggs to hatch and then, wide-eyed and tenderhearted, we watched the babies, barely born, heading for the sea, covering without hesitation the few yards separating them from the water. We learned that most of them would die in the next few hours, eaten by various predators, including sharks. Those that managed to reach the open sea and its depths would then have more chance of surviving. Statistically, out of the night's births, only one would survive in the end.

"Life is a lottery," said Claudia, angrily.

"Life is a perpetual race," her husband replied. "Only the fastest survive. Those who dawdle, flit around, or allow themselves pleasures die. You must always forge ahead."

I was stunned, as much by the baby turtles as by what I had just heard. It was extraordinary. In just a few words, each had summed up his vision of life. The last piece of the Dutch jigsaw puzzle was falling into place, giving meaning to all the scenes I had witnessed. I understood now why Claudia accepted the role of the housewife imposed by her husband: she had just drawn the unlucky number. When you've lost, you've lost; there's nothing you can do. You don't argue when you lose at the casino or the lottery. Things are as they are, and there's no point in wanting to change them. As for Hans, I understood better his obsession with action and his inability to allow himself moments of relaxation.

I wondered if turtles had beliefs about life as well, or if, on the contrary, the absence of beliefs allowed them in the end to live more in harmony with themselves.

I watched the baby turtles heading serenely for their natural element and wondered which would survive and come back here, in 50 years, when, in its turn, it had reached the age to give life.

10

THE RETURN TO my beach went smoothly, then I had my ritual swim, wondering what my career would be like if I were a baby turtle. Being naturally hesitant, I wondered if the expression "eaten up by doubt" wouldn't have taken on a very special meaning in this context.

After a very short night, I woke up quite early. I wanted sufficient time to gather the information that the healer had asked me to get before going to meet him, as quickly as possible.

In my guidebook, I located the nearest luxury hotel and jumped into my car. Twenty minutes later, I was driving slowly past the entrance to the Amankila, probably one of the most beautiful hotels in the world, and also one of the most intimate. I swallowed hard as I drove my cheap rental car into the hotel gardens, brutally aware of how out of place it was—and how dirty, especially after two weeks traipsing around the island's dusty roads. I slowly drove up the drive lined with opulent flower beds, hoping to make as little noise as possible, and parked as far as I could from reception. I went up the pretty path, zigzagging through a landscaped garden of exquisite refinement. I could see two gardeners on their knees on a lawn bordered by a rock garden. Each man was equipped with a pair of scissors, and they were conscientiously cutting the grass. In this kind of place, a vulgar lawn mower was out of the question; it would have disturbed the residents' tranquillity. I stood speechless for a moment before carrying on, trying to look natural, to imitate the nonchalance of a regular customer. It was difficult to keep up the pretense when the beauty of the sights before me almost took my breath away. A series of single-story buildings, partly without walls, built in contemporary colonial style, from precious materials, rare woods, beautiful stones, offering to the eye a gentle gradation of creams, looked onto the sea. Opposite them was a line of sublime infinity pools on three levels. The first was filled to the edge with water that flowed silently into the second below, which then flowed into the third. In a line, far off, was a spectacular view of the sea, of the same blue as the pools. They were so magnificently integrated into the landscape that it seemed like the sea itself had been painted to match them. Above, the blue immensity of the sky. A few coconut palms and other tropical trees were carefully laid out to reinforce the beauty and the perfection of the setting. I had the impression that nothing could be added or subtracted without spoiling this perfection. An absolute calm, no visible human presence. The residents no doubt preferred the intimacy of the private pools they each had in front of their suites, in elegant secluded gardens. Just a few employees, whose uniforms the color of undyed raw silk merged with the walls, made an occasional discreet, silent appearance, gliding like ghosts between the columns of the scattered buildings. I continued my way to the reception desk, finding it more and more difficult to feel at ease in this place. I was greeted by a distinguished man, in the same cream uniform, affable and smiling.

I put on a confident air.

"Hello, I'd like to access the Internet, please."

"Are you a hotel resident, sir?"

Why did he ask? He knew I wasn't. I had read in my guidebook that the hotel employed 200 people to look after 70 residents. Every day the employees learned by heart their names, which they used each time they met them. "How are you, Mr. Smith?" "Lovely day, isn't it, Mrs. Green?" "You're looking good today, Mr. King."

"No, I'm at the Legian," I lied, giving the name of another luxury hotel on the island. "I'm visiting here in the East, and I absolutely must connect to the Internet for a few minutes."

In any case, I doubted he would turn a Westerner away.

"Please follow me, sir."

He led me to an elegant room in which there was a computer already switched on, ready to welcome me. The room was almost as big as my apartment back home, with a hushed atmosphere, thick carpet on the floor, tropical wood paneling on the walls, a glass door with tiny panels, whose carved handle must have cost as much as my plane ticket.

It took me less than a quarter of an hour, following up the different suggestions from the search engine, to get the information I wanted.

What I read confirmed what the healer had rapidly sketched for me: pharmaceutical laboratories got together volunteers affected by an illness. They gave half of them the drug they had just produced to treat the illness and gave the other half a placebo, that is to say, a perfectly neutral, inactive substance that looked like medicine. These patients didn't know, of course, that they had been prescribed a placebo: they thought it was a drug supposed to cure their ailment. The scientists then measured the results from each of the two groups. To be able to demonstrate the effectiveness of their treatment, the patients who had taken the drug had to show results better than those from the group of people who had taken the placebo.

I discovered that the placebos had a certain impact on the illnesses, which was already extremely surprising, since they were real illnesses and the placebos were inactive substances. The only contribution was therefore psychological: the patients believed it was a drug and believed consequently that it was going to heal them. And, in certain cases, it was indeed enough to do so. What really made me sit up was the number of cases for which the belief in healing was enough to heal the patient. It was on average 30 percent! Even pains could disappear! A placebo was as effective as morphine in 54 percent of cases! Patients were in pain, they were suffering, and the taking of an ordinary sugar tablet or goodness knows what neutral ingredient stopped their pain. They just had to believe in it.

Dumbfounded, I went on checking a number of similar statistics concerning various illnesses. Then I came across the statistic that left me rooted to the spot, my fingers momentarily frozen to the keyboard: they had given patients a placebo that they were told was chemotherapy and 33 percent of them had completely lost their hair. I sat openmouthed in front of my screen. These patients had swallowed the equivalent of a lump of sugar, believing it was a drug whose well-known side effect is hair loss, and they had indeed lost their hair! But they had swallowed no more than a goddamned bit of sugar! I was stunned, astounded by this power of belief, which the healer had so insisted on. It was simply incredible. And yet, the figures were real, published by a laboratory famous for its chemotherapies. The moment after, weirdly, I felt somewhat indignant: Why weren't these statistics revealed to the public? Why not give them to the media? That would open debates that would, in the end, bring science to look at the question. If psychological phenomena made it possible to have such an effect on the body and illnesses, why concentrate research on the manufacture of costly drugs, which always had side effects? Why not give more attention to healing sickness by the psychological route?

I went out of the room, deliberately leaving the screen on the page giving this data. With a bit of luck, the next resident to come here would be the boss of a big newspaper group . . . There was no harm in dreaming.

I waved casually at the receptionist as I left, naturally without trying to pay for my Internet use: it would scarcely have seemed credible, coming from someone used to this sort of place.

11

"HELLO!" I SAID to the young woman, who welcomed me as usual.

It had taken me nearly an hour and a half to get here from the Amankila. Just the sight of the campan and its garden was enough to put me at once in a state of deep well-being, on a little cloud, a bit like when you open the bottle of sunblock from last summer and its perfume takes you back in an instant to the place of your last vacation.

"Master Samtyang isn't here today."

"Sorry?"

I was rudely brought back to Earth. Not here? This place and he were so inseparable that I found it hard to imagine he could be taken away from it.

"When will he be back? I'll wait for him."

"He told me to give you this," she said, holding out a beige sheet of paper folded in four.

He had left a message for me? If he wanted to

explain his absence, why hadn't he simply given a verbal message to the young woman so that she could pass it on to me? I unfolded the piece of paper and read it straight through, forgetting she was there:

Before our next meeting:

—Write down everything that is stopping you from achieving your dream of a happy life.
—Climb Mount Skouwo.

Samtyang

Climb Mount Skouwo? But that meant at least a four- or five-hour climb! And in this heat! Why not Annapurna?!

She watched me, smiling, not at all concerned by my worries.

"And did he say anything more when he gave you the message?" I asked.

"Nothing special. He just said to give it to you, adding that you would understand."

I understood above all that he wasn't here to meet me, when I only had three days left before my departure. I felt extremely frustrated.

"Do you know if he will be here tomorrow?"

"No doubt," she replied in a tone that meant she had no idea.

"If you see him, make sure you tell him that I'll be here tomorrow morning, and that

I'm really counting on him. I absolutely must see him."

I took my leave and returned reluctantly to my car.

Unenthusiastically, I set off in the direction of Mount Skouwo, in the north of the island. I mustn't delay if I wanted to climb it and get back down before night.

After a few miles, I saw a child walking by the roadside. He was eight or nine, I think—I've never been good at judging children's ages. As soon as he saw my car, he stopped and stuck out his thumb. I had no reason not to give him a lift. He got in, a smile of satisfaction on his face.

"What's your name?"

"Ketut."

Not surprising: there are only four Balinese first names, in the most common caste at any rate. When you meet a stranger, there is one chance in four that he's called Ketut.

"No school today?"

"No, not today."

"Are you going to your parents'?"

"My parents are both dead."

I shut up, annoyed at my gaffe, then I saw that he had kept his smile.

"They died in a car accident last week," he added, still smiling.

I was unsettled, even if I knew that the Balinese really don't have the same relationship to death that we do. Their belief in reincarnation makes them give it a very different meaning from ours. For them, death wasn't especially sad. I watched the child smile, and, for the first time, told myself that I would have liked to be Balinese and belong to a culture that would have produced such positive beliefs in me. For a long moment, I wondered what would be different about my life if I perceived my own death differently.

I dropped the child off at the next village and continued my journey.

Not a cloud to ease the heat of the sun. Climbing Mount Skouwo looked as though it was going to be painful. I really began to wonder if I was going to find the strength to do it. I didn't really feel like it, and in any case, I didn't see how it was meant to help me. Why had he given me this task? For what purpose? What was the link with our conversations, with my quest for a happy life? None. So, what was the point? And I had another task, a more relevant one. It would be better to concentrate on that.

The nearer I got to Mount Skouwo, the more I was looking for reasons not to climb it. I mustn't lie to myself, the healer had explained. Well, the truth was that I didn't at all want to do the climb. I didn't need to justify it with pseudorational arguments. I would tell the healer the truth tomorrow. And if I was supposed to discover something on the mountain, he would tell me what, and that would suffice. I am capable of understanding when things are explained to me.

At once I felt relieved by my decision, as though a weight had been taken off. I turned off at the next intersection and headed due east. Direction: my beach!

I arrived at the end of the afternoon. I parked and met Claudia as I walked to my bungalow.

"Hi, Claudia. Lovely day, isn't it?"

"Yes, it's nice today. We'll pay for it tomorrow," she said as she walked off.

The harmless sentences that I had always accepted without thinking tickled my ears now. Claudia's world was rather sad, so good things were dodgy. Perhaps she thought she didn't deserve them, and when one came along, she expected to pay the price sooner or later.

I armed myself with a notebook and a pencil, and sat on the sand, leaning against the trunk of a palm tree, taking advantage of its light shade. The beach was deserted; just one little fishing boat, out at sea, betrayed a human presence between me and the infinity of the horizon.

I began by noting all that had come to mind, the evening before, at the restaurant. I felt I was writing my happiness will. If I happened to die, my heirs could read the life I would have liked to have.

What was stopping me from leading that desired life? It was difficult to give an overall answer. I had to get down to details. I reviewed one by one the points I had mentioned, and unfortunately it was easy to find the reasons that made it impossible to carry out my dreams, follow my plans, achieve my ideas, and, finally, reach happiness.

I spent nearly an hour writing, and I felt quite melancholic as I watched night falling over the sea afterward. Like everyone, I'd had moments of happiness, but I had the feeling that I wasn't made for living fully happy. Happiness was perhaps reserved for certain people, for a few elect that didn't include me.

The time for my night swim arrived, and I swam in silence for a very long time.

Getting up early was becoming a habit. I absolutely wanted to see the healer that day, and I was slightly apprehensive because of his absence the day before. I got ready quickly and jumped into my car without forgetting the notes I had taken. I did a little speeding and entertained myself with the thought that running over a pedestrian or two would give them a chance of being reincarnated sooner than planned.

I was relieved to hear myself being told "please follow me" when I reported to the young woman at the entrance to the campan. I relaxed, breathed in the garden's perfumed air, and it was with genuine joy that I greeted Master Samtyang when he joined me.

"I was very disappointed not to see you yesterday," I confessed.

"Have you made progress with your thoughts about your life?"

"Yes."

"You see? You don't need me that much," he said with a smile.

We sat on the floor, on the mat, as usual.

"So, did you find interesting information about placebos?" he asked me.

"Yes, and what I read astounded me," I admitted.

I told him the results of my research the day before in Amankila. "I thought I would find proof of the effect of placebos on illnesses in which the mind plays an obvious role, like sleep disorders, for example. But I was really surprised to discover their impact on 'palpable' illnesses, and even the effects they can have directly on the body. It's very impressive," I said.

"Yes, it's true."

"I thought it was a shame that more research isn't done into using the mechanism of beliefs to heal people."

"Yes, especially as it isn't new. Two thousand years ago, Jesus was doing it already."

"I'm sorry?"

"It's never talked about, but Jesus used people's beliefs to heal them."

"You're joking. Are you planning to write *Da Vinci Code 3*?"

Without replying, he leaned toward the

little camphor-wood chest, and, to my astonishment, brought out a Bible.

"Are you a Christian?"

"No, but that doesn't stop a person from being interested in the Bible."

He calmly flicked through the pages and then read me a passage. "Jesus is replying to some blind people who are begging him to heal them—it's from Matthew 9, verses 28 and 29: 'Jesus said unto them, "Believe ye that I am able to do this?" They said unto him, "Yea, Lord." Then touched he their eyes, saying, "According to your faith be it unto you."'"

"Did he really say that?"

"Read it for yourself," he said holding out the opened Bible. "You will notice that he doesn't say, 'I, all-powerful Jesus, have the ability to heal you.' No, he asks if they believe he has that power, then he tells them they will obtain what they believe in. It's very different."

I couldn't get over it. I read over and over again the passage from Saint Matthew's Gospel. It was incredible. How could Jesus know what practically nobody in the 21st century knew? How could he understand to that extent the working of human beings deep down inside themselves? I had to admit I was disturbed by what I had just discovered.

The healer's voice brought me back to Earth.

"An American researcher recently carried out a survey into the effectiveness of all the various cancer treatments. He examined the results from one group of patients. As the results were quite disparate, this led him to carry his investigation further. In the end he revealed that, in this group, the patients who got better had undergone very different treatments from one another. On the other hand, these patients all had one thing in common."

"What?"

"All those who got better were absolutely convinced beforehand that their treatment was going to heal them. They had total confidence in their doctors and the choice of treatment. For them, getting better was a given."

"So, the treatment doesn't matter—what counts is believing in it?"

"In a way."

"It's crazy. Yet cancer isn't a psychosomatic illness. And its presence in the body can be observed undeniably."

"All the possible causes of cancer are not yet well known. There is probably a hereditary factor, environmental causes, pollution, diet, et cetera. But perhaps there also exists, in certain cases, a psychological dimension that is still unrecognized."

"How's that?"

"A few years ago, something disturbing happened that no one could explain."

"What?"

"A woman showing all the symptoms of a blood cancer, a leukemia, was admitted to the ER of an

American hospital. A blood sample was immediately taken that showed a blood analysis typical of leukemia. The hospital procedures required a second sample be taken to confirm the results of the first. Now, the second blood sample showed a perfectly normal blood analysis. Surprised, the doctors asked for a third sample. That time, the results were identical to those of the first test. So the doctors thought that the second blood test was badly done and its results were wrong. To be sure, they ordered a fourth blood sample. Except that one confirmed the results of . . . the second one. Amazement and incomprehension. It was only later that they learned that the patient suffered from a split personality. She was capable of changing personality from one moment to the next. And it turned out that this change had taken place between the different blood samples. One of her personalities had cancer, not the other."

"But it was the same person!"

"Yes."

"It's unbelievable!"

"It's a mystery. No one's ever been able to explain it."

I was impressed and again enthusiastic about the idea that, when research was done in this area, the field of what was possible in medicine would be considerably enlarged.

"To bring this chapter on health to an end," he said, "it is interesting to know that people who believe in God and practice their religion, whatever it is, regularly have a life expectancy twenty-nine percent higher than the others."

"You know, nothing surprises me anymore!"

"As I was saying to you last time, you can't judge a belief, but you can take an interest in its effects. In this case, no one can prove the existence of God, but we know that one of the effects of the belief in God is a lengthened lifespan."

"Well, perhaps I'll go back to church on Sunday!"

"I'm not sure that would do any good. It's the belief that counts, not the behavior, even if—and ecclesiastics know this for a fact—rituals keep belief alive. By the way, what is that medallion you are wearing?"

"This?" I said, pointing to the little cross hung round my neck.

"Yes."

"My father gave it to me while he was still alive, 'to bring me happiness,' he said. I'm very attached to it because it comes from him."

"Many people believe so strongly in their lucky charm that they wouldn't go out without it. What's more, I wouldn't advise them to . . ."

I was going to get sticky food yet again. It was with a forced smile, and thinking about how to avoid it without annoying anyone, that I saw the young woman's tray arrive.

"That's very kind of you, but I don't want to abuse your hospitality."

"It's a pleasure for us to offer it to you," she said, to my discomfort.

I felt obliged to accept.

"Oh, then I'll just have a tiny bit, because I've already had a lot to eat this morning."

She held out a plate to me, served Master Samtyang, and disappeared. He had seen my embarrassment and was displaying a broad smile. He was having great fun.

"Why did you lie again?"

I wasn't going to deny it and get tied up in more lies. In any case, there would have been no point: this man could read my thoughts.

"So as not to annoy you by saying that I don't like your food and hate eating in the Balinese manner, getting my hands sticky—"

"If I can't understand that and get annoyed, it's my problem, not yours."

"Sorry?"

"It's not the message that annoys, but the means of transmitting it, of expressing it. If you're tactful, for example, if you thank the other person for their positive intention, you don't annoy them. Or else, they are particularly sensitive and then, in a way, it's *their* problem, not yours."

"You know, I think I also acted like that because it was easier than explaining the truth."

"Now you're mildly deceiving yourself. When

you don't tell people the truth, you tempt them to get around your arguments, which leads you to lie again. That's what happened, incidentally. In the end, you find yourself forced to do something against your will, like eating food you don't like. So you're doubly punished."

"Doubly?"

"Yes, because, first and foremost, lying is bad for you. It's a little bit as though it generates negative energy that builds up in you. Try the truth. You'll see that it's liberating, and you feel a lot lighter all at once."

Light was a convincing word, a desirable promise when you were choking on bland, gluey food.

"Speaking of truth, I didn't follow your instruction yesterday: I didn't go up Mount Skouwo."

"I'm not surprised."

"I didn't feel like it, so I didn't."

"And what effect does simply telling the truth have on you?"

"I admit it's pleasant. It's a sweet sensation."

"Good. Did you carry out the other tasks I gave you?"

"Yes, I wrote down my vision of an ideal life, then I wrote down everything that was preventing me from carrying it out."

I got my notes out and read to him the description of the life that I dreamed of. He listened in silence, and it was a pleasant feeling, having someone pay attention to my desires without commenting on them, without breaking in to dissuade me or suggesting something better in his opinion. I had heard so many saboteurs of dreams, those people who say, "If I were you, I'd . . . ," or, even worse, those who predict negative consequences for your ideas: "If you do that, you'll . . ."

When I'd finished, he just asked me, after a silence, "How do you know that life would make you happy?"

"I feel it. I've imagined it several times, and each time I have the same feeling, the same satisfaction. Especially, when I imagine myself living that, I have no other desires."

"And when you see yourself living this life, is there anything you might lose in relation to your present situation?"

"Nothing, absolutely nothing."

"Perfect. Before going into details, I'd just like to know your feeling about the reason why the life you describe isn't yours at present. What might have brought about the fact that your path is, overall, different from the one you would have liked to follow?"

"For starters, I think I don't have much luck in general. To make a success of your life, you must have luck, and I'm not very lucky—"

"You were saying just now that you weren't religious," he said with a laugh, "but you are superstitious! I don't believe in luck. I believe that everyone meets a great number of all sorts of opportunities in his life, and some people know how to recognize them and grab hold of them—others not."

"Perhaps."

"A very amusing experiment was carried out recently, in Europe, if my memory serves me well. It put volunteers, some of whom said they were lucky and others not, through a test. Each one was given a newspaper and a few minutes to count the precise number of photos printed inside. After a few pages, a fairly large insert appeared in the middle of the paper, saying in very large letters, 'There's no point in carrying on counting: there are 46 photos in the paper.'

"The people who thought they were lucky all stopped when they read this message. They closed the paper and said to the researcher, 'There are 46 photos.' In your opinion, what did the people who said they were unlucky do?"

"I don't know. I would say they thought there must be a trap somewhere, and they continued counting to the end to be sure, before giving the number?"

"No. It's true they continued counting to the end of the paper, but, when they were asked why they hadn't taken account of the insert, they all said, 'An insert? What insert?' None of them had seen it!"

"Interesting, indeed."

"Yes, I'm convinced that you have as much luck

as everybody else, but perhaps you don't pay attention to the opportunities that present themselves to you."

"It's possible."

Again I wondered what opportunities I had let slip past in my life and what would have been its course if I had seen them and grabbed hold of them.

"Right, now, let's go over the different elements of your dream."

"The central element is to work for myself by setting up my own wedding-photo studio."

"Good. So tell me, what is preventing you?"

"Actually, I'm afraid of not being able to, even though this plan attracts me enormously."

"How do you know you wouldn't be able to?"

"I can feel it: it's so different from my present job, from what I'm used to doing. Perhaps it's too big a change and I won't manage."

"If you just rely on a feeling, you don't have any way of knowing if it's reality or just a limiting belief."

"Perhaps."

"Do you know how you begin to believe you're not capable of something?"

"No."

"When there exists a question somewhere, often not consciously expressed, to which you don't have the answer."

"I'm not following you."

"An example: if you don't know the answer to

the question 'How can I concretely carry out this plan?' then you risk thinking, *I'm not capable of carrying it out,* which is a limiting belief. So, I'm asking you how you intend to set about making this plan see the light of day."

"I don't know."

"You see? As long as you haven't answered that question, you will have the feeling of not being capable of realizing your dream."

"I understand."

"To answer it, you will have to get down more to the details, because, as long as you keep a global image of your plan, you will see it as an abstract thing, therefore unachievable."

"It's true; I have emotions, but no precise action plan. Positive emotions when I dream of the result, negative when I think of going into action."

"There you are. You will demystify the plan by making a precise list of everything you will have to do to achieve it, then noting for each task what you can do and what you can't yet do. Then all you have to do is find out how to get the skills you lack."

"There are quite a lot of things I will have to learn that are completely foreign to me today—for example, how to manage what is, after all, to a certain extent a small business. I'll need commercial skills, since I will have to make myself known and sell my services. The problem is that I have neither the time nor the money to get training."

"Right, you can also call on your creativity: it's not always necessary to have lessons to learn to do something! For example, who are the people around you who might have the skills you don't have and might pass them on to you?"

My principal has some of them, but of course it's out of the question to talk to him about it."

"Who else, then?"

"My old principal, in the school where I taught before."

"Perfect. You'll be able to ask him to help you."

"No . . ."

"What's stopping you?"

"It doesn't feel right."

"Why?"

"I don't know. I don't want to trouble him with my problems."

"How do you know it would trouble him?" he asked me, astonished, as if I had just told him I was a mind reader, able to know in advance what people were going to think.

"He probably won't want to waste time helping someone he isn't close to or who isn't a member of his family."

"If it were you, wouldn't you help someone who came to ask you for advice about a job?"

"Yes, yes, of course I would."

He looked right at me.

"What are you afraid of, then?" he asked me with infinite gentleness.

Once again, I had the impression that he was putting his finger exactly in the right place, so that he didn't need to press hard to produce an effect. The word *fear* caused a particular echo in me. For a few moments, it rang like a gong in my rib cage, and the vibrations went down deep into the recesses of my mind. What came back up to the surface appeared self-evident.

"I'm afraid of being told to get lost, so I prefer not to risk it."

Just thinking about it, I could feel the shame I would experience if my ex-boss told me where I could get off.

"Your fear comes from confusing the rejection of a request and the rejection of a person. It's not because your request is refused that you are not liked or someone doesn't have regard for you."

"Perhaps."

"Plus, you absolutely don't know if his reaction would be negative. You can't answer for people. It's only by asking the question that you'll know for sure."

"I'm probably not enough of a masochist."

"Most of our fears are created by our minds. You probably don't understand, but knowing how to turn to others to ask them something is fundamental. All the people who make a success of their lives have that ability."

"Perhaps I have others that make up for the one I haven't got—"

"You absolutely must acquire it. You can't go far in life without being able to ask others for support, backing, help, advice, contacts. Before we say good-bye today, I will give you a task to help you progress in this area."

I accepted, praying that it wouldn't involve climbing another mountain or swimming across a bay, weaving in and out of sharks.

"With regard to what I must learn to get my plan off the ground, there is something that may pose a problem."

"What?"

"It's impossible to run a studio on your own, particularly because, when you are out on a job, there's nobody to look after customers or answer the phone. So I would have to take on one or two people. That's where things get awkward."

"What do you mean?"

"Well, if there is one thing I'm afraid I'm really not cut out for, it's managing people."

"How do you know that?" he asked, looking slightly amused.

"My principal had to be away for a day, and he asked me to replace him so that, if necessary, there was someone in charge in the school. And, as though on purpose, it happened. One of my colleagues was taken ill while teaching, and I had to allocate his pupils to the other classes. But each class had its own timetable, and the pupils I entrusted to each teacher had to stay to the time scheduled in their original class. Some teachers protested, refusing to do overtime that wasn't planned in advance. I had to try to negotiate with each of them. To no avail. It ended in a nightmare: I gathered all the pupils together in my classroom, which was too small to take everyone in. Some started crying. I wasn't in control; it was a mess. The next day, I could read the contempt on my principal's face. I told myself I would never try to manage people again."

"You had difficulties in this area on one occasion, and you conclude that you're not meant for it."

"More than just difficulties: failure."

"You never tried again?"

"I was careful not to."

"Have you ever looked at a baby learning to walk?"

"Thanks for the comparison."

"Babies have an enormous amount to teach us. Watch a baby learning to walk: you think he succeeds at the first attempt? He tries to stand up, and—oops!—down he goes. It's a total failure, and yet he starts again straightaway. He stands up again and . . . down he goes! A baby will fall on average two thousand times before he can walk."

He smiled and added, "If every baby were like you, towns would be swarming with people crawling on all fours."

"In a word, you're telling me that I've come up

with yet another little limiting belief on the basis of one failure."

"Yes, and no doubt you need to do a proper management training course."

"As I said, that would take time and money, and I don't have much of either."

"I don't think it costs more than a vacation in Bali."

"I don't like interfering with my vacations or my weekends. For me, time off is sacred."

"It's for you to choose which is more important: fulfilling your dream or taking advantage of your time off," he said in a perfectly neutral tone that left me free to make up my mind.

"I want to fulfill my dream, but it would be tough to go without my vacations!"

"You said that fulfilling this dream would make you happy. Do vacations make you happy?"

"That would be saying a lot. Let's say they give me pleasure, and I'm attached to them."

"There are circumstances where you have to make choices, and therefore give up things you like, to go toward things that mean more," he said quite simply.

"I hate giving anything up."

"If you give nothing up, you are refraining from making choices. And when you refrain from choosing, you refrain from living the life you want."

He said that gently, his eyes full of goodness. As someone who had often felt that avoiding decisions was sparing himself suffering, I now felt I was contributing to my own unhappiness in this way.

"Don't get me wrong," he went on. "I'm not trying to convince you not to have holidays anymore. I just want you to be aware that you can't fulfill the dream of your life if you're not prepared to exert yourself and, if necessary, make a few sacrifices."

Of course, it seemed common sense, and yet one doesn't become capable of effort and sacrifice on the basis of a simple decision. I felt that some people were born like that, endowed with this ability. That was clearly not my case.

"Following one's path in order to be able to fulfill oneself completely is sometimes like climbing a mountain. Until you've done it, you don't know that the effort it demands increases the satisfaction you feel on arrival. The greater the effort is, the more intense the happiness and the longer it will remain engraved in you."

I got the message loud and clear, and was grateful to him for not having explicitly commented on my avoidance of the climb up Mount Skouwo.

"I will have to find a means," he said, as if he was talking to himself, "of making you consider choice, effort, and sacrifice."

I was so lucky to have this man interested in me to the point of thinking about how to get around my failures to keep my commitments, which he was doing so that, in spite of everything, I could learn what I had to learn!

"We'll leave it there for today," he went on, "but for tomorrow, I'd like you to project yourself forward a few months, imagining that you have finally got all the skills you lack at the moment. I want you to put yourself in the shoes of a photographer and tell me how you feel."

"Right."

"One last thing: I had promised to give you a task to carry out in order to rid you of this fear of going up to people to ask them for help, this fear of being rejected."

"Yes."

"Right, here you are: we will meet again tomorrow, and by then you will have gone up to people of your choice and asked them things, anything, but with one goal in mind."

"Which is?"

"Getting a negative response from them."

"I'm sorry?"

"You heard me: you must take steps so that the people you ask reject your request. More precisely, you must make them clearly say no to you. They must say that word. And your task is to obtain five no's by tomorrow."

"That shouldn't be too difficult."

"Then have fun. I'll expect you here tomorrow morning," he said, making as though he was leaving.

"Just one thing: I'm leaving Bali on Saturday to go home."

"Already? I had intended to see you three or four more times."

"That's possible tomorrow and Friday, but on Saturday I've got my plane in the afternoon. Or perhaps we could meet in the morning?"

"On Saturdays, I'm not available in the morning."

"Really?"

"If you want us to meet one last time on Saturday, all you have to do is change your ticket and go home Sunday!" he said, as though it were obvious.

"That's not so easy. The type of ticket I've got has a hefty surcharge for any change of date. And I go back to work on Monday. The flight is so long I would have to go directly from the airport to my class. I'd rather avoid—"

"We'll see tomorrow if there are still important things left for you to discover and if it's really necessary to see each other again on Saturday."

I WAS SUDDENLY very aware of what little time I had left before my departure, and I wanted to get things done without delay. I had understood during this session that the tasks he gave me to do between meetings were not meaningless, and now I had my heart set on achieving those he had set for me that day.

Admittedly, I was not enthusiastic about the idea of doing what I hated: going up to people to ask them to do something for me, but I was curious to see what I would get out of it in the end, since—I was sure of this now—everything the healer asked me to do had a purpose.

So I went to Ubud, a place where I knew I could find Westerners. Going up to Balinese would have been a waste of time; they didn't know how to say no.

How was I going to start? I had to formulate

requests in such a way that they would be refused. In short, I had to make sure I ended with the result that, normally, I took great care to avoid. So, five times, I was going to hear the final *no* of people dismissing me. Great.

The main street was fairly lively in the midafternoon. Perfect: I would be able to hide my repeated disgraces more easily.

"Taxi! Taxi!" Balinese were calling to tourists all over the place. One of them spoke to me.

"I haven't any money on me. Can you take me to Kuta for free?" I said with a laugh.

"It's fifty thousand rupiahs. You can pay on the way back," he said with a broad smile.

"No, I have no money. Can you make it a present?"

"Okay, you're nice. For you, it's thirty thousand rupiahs."

"No. For free. A present."

"Okay, twenty thousand rupiahs."

"No, I can't."

"Look, we'll go to Kuta, and we'll discuss the fare. We'll reach an agreement. Come on, in you get!"

"No, it's okay. I'll go some other way, thank you."

I was more and more embarrassed.

"Come on, get in. We'll come to some agreement."

"It's okay, thanks—thanks a lot."

"Come on!"

"No, thank you, I've changed my mind. I'm not going to Kuta anymore. Bye."

He watched me walk away, amused, as though to say, "These Westerners are really weird."

Right, one attempt wasted. I had heard five *no's,* but I was saying them! In any case, why had I gone up to a Balinese, when I'd decided that was pointless? No doubt because it was easy. The Balinese were very mild and very nice, and they put me more at ease than my compatriots and their neighbors. I had to face the obvious: I was so afraid of being rejected that I preferred to increase the difficulty of the exercise rather than face my fear. Come on, I was going to summon up my courage, face my anxiety, quickly get my five *no's,* and run and hide on my deserted beach.

I looked around. There were numerous people on the narrow pavement of the main street. Some were coming out of art galleries, while others were going into magnificent cafés whose postcolonial design was clearly aimed at Westerners. People were taking care as they walked not to trample the offerings scattered on the ground.

I had to take the plunge, even if it meant randomly choosing someone and asking the first thing that popped into my mind. Then I spotted a large American woman in a turquoise skirt and a pink blouse. She was coming out of an ice cream parlor, holding a large cone overflowing with ice cream.

"What a magnificent ice cream!" I said to her.

"Delicious!" she replied, her eyes gleaming.

Her lips were shining, slicked by the ice cream.

"Can I have a lick?" I forced myself to ask.

"Oh, aren't you bold!" she said, her eyes sparkling.

I could read in her eyes that letting me put my lips on the ice cream was virtually tantamount to having me kiss her.

"Can I, or can't I?"

"Of course you can, darling," she replied, coming closer and looking at me hungrily.

"No, I was joking, I was joking," I said, making myself laugh.

"Don't be afraid—you can have a lick. Go on."

"No, thank you, I just said it for nothing . . . for nothing. Right, so long. Enjoy your ice cream!"

I left her standing there in disbelief, her fingers frozen on her cone, the ice cream slowly running down her hand.

Another failure. With collateral damage. I was bright red, and I was angry with myself for perhaps having offended someone. I walked faster and turned off down the first side street I came across, so I could take a few moments to gather my scattered wits. I was wondering what my next request would be, when I saw on a wooden gate a notice announcing PRINGGA JUWITA. I walked forward and saw through the dense vegetation the bungalows of a hotel hidden under the trees.

I was going up to it when two tourists walked out of the gate.

"Excuse me," I said, "are you staying in the hotel?"

"Yes."

"I'm staying on the east side of the island. My car has just broken down, and it won't be repaired until tomorrow. I have absolutely no money on me to stay in a hotel. I know my request is out of place, but would you by any chance allow me to sleep in your room tonight? I don't want to spend the night outside."

They looked at each other in surprise for a moment, then one of them said, "Your car's broken down?"

"Yes."

"You didn't ask the garage man to put you up?"

"No."

"People are very hospitable here; he can perhaps accommodate you or recommend you to one of his neighbors. I'd like to, but our room is quite small. Do you want me to ask at the hotel? We've been here for a week, and they're beginning to know us. I know they're full, but I'm sure they would know someone who could put up a friend of one of their customers."

"No, I'll manage, thank you. It's very kind of you."

"As you wish."

"Thanks all the same."

"Best of luck."

"Thanks. Bye-bye."

Heavens, couldn't they just have said no? As I watched them disappear around the corner, I began to have the impression that it was going to be harder than I thought.

Another tourist left the hotel at that moment, and I was preparing to repeat my request when I stopped in my tracks: I was suddenly afraid that he might hear my words as a proposition.

I retraced my steps to the main street. Still as many people. I must find something so outrageous that people would be obliged to refuse. Let's think, let's think, let's think . . . money. Yes, that's it, money. As soon as you hit their pocket, people get wary and become a lot more direct.

I passed the entrance to the post office and went up to the first person who came out. She was in her 50s, gray hair cut very short, somewhat masculine-looking—the assertive type who has no difficulty saying no. The ideal prey. I already liked her.

"Forgive me for troubling you, but I really need to make an important phone call abroad. I've no money on me. Would you be so kind as to give me five hundred rupiahs so that I can phone from the post office?"

"You've got an urgent call to make?" she asked in a fairly authoritarian way.

"Yes."

"Where are you calling?"

She was looking me straight in the face with a frown.

"The States."

"Will you be long?"

It felt a bit like being questioned by the police.

"Yes, five minutes, perhaps six."

"Follow me to my hotel," she ordered. "It's just next door. I use the hotel phone with a prepaid card, which costs next to nothing. But you can use it for three minutes exactly, no more."

"Unfortunately, that's not going to be enough. Could you allow six minutes?"

I didn't recognize myself. I would never have had the audacity to ask for that before, especially from a lady who was being so extremely kind as to grant three minutes of her phone card to help out a stranger.

"I'm sure you'll manage in three minutes. Come on!" she said, pulling me along. "You'll learn to be concise. It's very useful in life!"

Honestly, everyone wanted to give me advice about my life.

"No, but . . . I don't want to put you out by going to your hotel. Don't worry, I'll manage."

"You're not putting me out," she affirmed, in an authoritative voice, continuing to advance, show-ing me the way.

"But you'll probably need it yourself. I don't want to eat into your phone credit."

"Come on. If it were a problem, I wouldn't have offered."

Ten minutes later, I was calling my home number to have a rushed dialogue with my answering machine. I hung up after two minutes.

"You were right: two minutes was long enough."

"Perfect! Right. Your problem's sorted out?" she asked like the perfect know-it-all.

"Yes, I don't know how to thank you."

"In that case, don't try!"

"Right then . . . good-bye—enjoy the rest of your stay!"

"Good-bye and remember: in life you need to know how to aim straight at the goal!"

She watched me walk off and, when I turned around ten yards further on, was smiling, obviously pleased with herself—and a long way from imagining that she had acted contrary to my wishes.

Dejected, I went into the first café I saw, which was called Yogi's, to have a cool drink. At this rate, it would take me a week to get my five *no's*. It was depressing. Once I was through the door, the tranquillity contrasted sharply with my weariness and at once enveloped me in a feeling of well-being. The light subdued by elegant wooden venetian blinds, low armchairs, low tables, music by Sha'aban Yahya quietly playing, customers speaking in hushed tones—this was the ideal place to stay for a few minutes and recharge my batteries. I ordered an iced tea as

I sank into one of the armchairs, allowing the built-up tension to drop. I let my eyelids close for a few moments and freed the air in my lungs in a long, silent sigh. I had the impression I'd forgotten to breathe for an hour. The new air I inhaled cooled my nostrils, and the sweetness of its mixed perfumes of tea and incense soothed me. Well-being spread in me, running along my respiratory system to its tiniest ramifications. I stayed awhile like this, as though weightless, emptying my mind.

When I opened my eyes again, I saw a young woman, like an apparition, sitting on a pouf a few yards away from me. I would have sworn she wasn't there when I came in—unless she was already there and the torment in my mind had made her invisible until I relaxed. She was very thin, and her narrow back, which I was seeing in profile, showed a pronounced natural curve. Her long brown hair was tied at the neck, showing enough of it for me to see how delicate it was. She was absorbed in a book that was resting on a low table, and her right hand was mechanically stirring the little spoon in the cup of steaming tea. I observed her for a long time, admiring her natural grace. She broke off to raise the cup to her lips, pretty, full lips that made me think of a raspberry. She put the cup back down, delicately turning her head in my direction, and her eyes settled on me as if, aware of my presence, she had been waiting for the right moment to pay attention to me. Her eyes met mine and didn't turn away for a time that seemed an eternity. My eyes were so caught up in hers that I didn't even dare blink anymore. I had the impression that the distance that separated us was lessening, as though someone were using a zoom lens and all that was around us had become blurred or disappeared. I was surrounded by nothingness before the eye of a cyclone of beauty that was sucking me in, like a black hole. The background music seemed a long way away, and at the same time, it could have been coming from inside me. The young woman was not smiling, and her face was perfectly motionless. Only her delicate nostrils rose imperceptibly in time with her breathing. It would have been futile to try to decipher her thoughts, to understand what her eyes meant. What we were experiencing was beyond thought, beyond language, beyond understanding. Her soul was speaking to my soul, which was answering. It concerned only them, and it was pointless to seek a meaning for something that was bigger than us. In any case, I wanted nothing, needed nothing. I was no longer me; I was beyond me. I had perhaps reached, for a few moments, that dimension where people join together and commune without speaking.

I experienced such a distortion of time that I was unable afterward to know how long it had lasted. The contact was broken by a waiter who brought the bill and struck up a conversation. After I took the time to reply, to look for my money, to pay, to get the change . . . she was no longer there. She had disappeared as she had appeared. I felt it was futile to look for her, to rush outside, to ask the people present. Finding her again, making contact, talking to her, all that would just have brought back to a terrestrial level what we had experienced on a more spiritual level. And then, nothing can be added to perfection without spoiling it, drawing away from it, and finally losing it. And, besides, perfection cannot be the basis for a relationship. Nothing can be built on it. Life is anything but perfection.

I remained a little while in Yogi's before remembering my task. I went out and spent the following hour going up to various people to make different types of requests, getting ever more outrageous. And yet, never did I manage to get an outright, massive *no*. Either people partially met my request or they tried to find an indirect way of nonetheless satisfying the need I expressed. I felt that I was going to end the day disappointed, though I had really intended to succeed with my task . . . Fortunately, at the corner of the street, I suddenly saw the person who was going to save my honor and keep me from going home empty-handed.

"Hans! Hans!" I called from a way off. "Hans, could you lend me some money?"

14

I WENT BACK to the bungalow savoring this easy victory. It was the first time in my life that I was filled with pleasure at seeing a face in the act of closing up, seeing the eyes freeze, the brow knit into a deep line above the nose, the lips tighten.

It had seemed that the scene was taking place in slow motion—extreme slow motion—allowing me to enjoy each thousandth of a second, image by image, and I remember each one of them as though it were yesterday: I can see his mouth open again and, at the precise instant that the tongue left the palate, his breathing had given off a sharp noise that had cracked in the air like a whip, forming the magic word of rejection, the word I had desperately sought to collect all afternoon. I could have filmed the scene to play it back in a loop.

I had almost lifted my arms and looked up to the sky as I fell on my knees, like tennis champions who have just won match point in the final of a grand-slam contest. I could have thrown my arms around his neck and kissed him with gratitude. I made do with smiling and looking at him in silence, awaiting the pleasure of seeing him justify his position with a phony excuse or two-bit moral. When I said it was a joke, he had laughed, with the forced laugh of someone who is relieved but has kept the contraction brought on by the initial request.

Borne along by my victory, I had scored a second point while I was at it by phoning the travel agency in Kuta, where I was clearly told *no,* it wasn't possible to change my plane ticket without paying a penalty of $600. I had never received such bad news in such a good mood.

In the enthusiasm of the moment, I had managed to contact my former principal. I hadn't worked out the time difference and had the impression I was getting him out of bed. His voice was sleepy, with the hint of anxiety you have when the phone rings in the middle of the night and you wonder what terrible news can justify being dragged out of sleep at such an hour. I talked to him enthusiastically about my plan, without paying attention to the contrast between my excitement and his sleepiness. He listened to me, and when I asked him if he would consent to give me a little of his time to teach me different aspects of his know-how, he agreed, no doubt relieved that I wasn't calling to announce the death of his grandmother or the explosion of his school in a terrorist attack.

In the end, two out of five seemed an honorable score for a beginner, and I went back to my beach confident and calm, and spent the evening on my second task: imagining myself in the shoes of a photographer and listening to my feelings in this new professional identity.

My nocturnal swim was a delicious time of letting go, of relaxation and happiness after the harassing but victorious day.

15

"So, WAS IT as easy as you imagined to get those *no's?*"

"Well, no, I have to admit it wasn't."

He smiled as he sat down on the mat in the lotus position. I looked at him, happy to be opposite him again. I liked his serene, imperturbable face—the face of someone who expects nothing more from life, who covets nothing, has no particular desires. Someone who is happy just to be and who offers that state to others as a model to be followed if they wish.

"People who are afraid of being rejected," he went on, "have no idea that it is rare to be turned down by others. It's difficult to bring about. On the whole, people are inclined to help you, not to disappoint you, to go along with what you expect from them. It's precisely when you are afraid of being rejected that, in the end, you are—according to the belief mechanism that you have learned to know now."

"It's true."

"When you learn to go toward others to ask them for what you need, a whole world offers itself to you. Life is about opening up to others, not closing up on oneself. Anything that allows you to connect to others is positive."

I thought back to my connection with Hans the day before. After all, it had been a good moment, and in the end, I had recognized that he was more to be pitied than despised.

"I think you're right."

"So did you manage to imagine yourself in the shoes of the person you are thinking of becoming?"

"Well, as it happens, I wanted to talk to you about that. I've got a problem."

"It's good to have become aware of it before launching into the plan."

"Yes, you're right."

"What's your problem?"

"When I imagine myself in the shoes of a photographer, that's to say, an artist, I don't feel completely at ease with the idea."

"What bothers you exactly?" he asked in a way that invited me to confide in him.

"Well, I'm from . . . how should I say . . . a family that values only the intellectual professions. My parents pushed me to go into higher education. I would even say that I didn't have a choice.

In my family, you are respected if you are a scientist or a teacher—that's about all. Other forms of employment are not thought of as worthy. So, a photographer—"

"They are entitled to their opinions, and you are entitled to do what you want with your life."

"Of course, and it's obvious that at my age I don't owe them an explanation, but it would come as such a shock! I'm worried they'd be upset."

"Are they upset, today, to know that you are not happy in your job? Have they been a comfort to you?"

"No, not really."

"If they love you, which do you think they prefer: that you're an unhappy teacher or a happy photographer?"

"Looking at it that way—"

"That's how you must look at it: if we love people only when they behave in conformity with our ideals, it's not love. I think you have nothing to fear from those who love you. Even in a loving family, everyone must live his own life. It's good to consider the effects of what we do on others so as not to hurt them. On the other hand, you can't always take their wishes into account, and even less the way they're going to judge your actions. Each one of us is responsible for judging himself. You're not responsible for other people's opinions."

He was no doubt right, but something was still bothering me. "In fact, I wonder to what extent my family might have 'contaminated' me: even if I am enthusiastic about this plan, I'm not completely relaxed about the idea of leaving the intellectual camp to join the artistic one!"

"I think it's inappropriate to think in terms of camps, even more of belonging to a camp. For you, it's not a question of leaving one camp to join another, but just of carrying out a plan that is dear to you."

I remained pensive, definitely affected by his words, but I think he felt the situation still left me with a mental block.

"Come with me," he said, slowly getting up.

From the way he moved, for the first time, I became aware of his great age, an impression that disappeared when he spoke, because he used words with such precision and calm.

I got up and followed him. He went around the different buildings that made up the campan, then took a path that wound through vegetation so dense that you couldn't make out the outlines of the garden. We walked for several minutes in silence, one behind the other, then the path widened and I walked beside him. Minute plots had been placed here and there, and were carefully cultivated, probably with medicinal plants; some of them had microscopic yellow or blue flowers. After crossing a thicket of giant, bushy bamboos with a green smell, plunging us into semidarkness and enveloping us in damp humidity, the path suddenly came out on a ledge with a breathtaking drop down to the valley. I had known the village was perched high up, but I never imagined that the end of Master Samtyang's garden so dominated the valley that stretched for miles, 200 or 300 yards below. This plunging, aerial view—it was as though we were suspended over a void—contrasted strongly with the rest of the garden, where the density of the vegetation prevented a clear view. We sat down side by side on a rock, our feet swinging in the void, and stayed silent for several minutes, contemplating the grandiose landscape, which made me feel very small. It was the healer who in the end broke the silence with his calm, kindly voice.

"What can you see in the rice fields?"

Far off, down below, were dozens of workers standing in water up to their calves, their backs bent and their hands reaching toward the rice plants.

"I see a series of workers active in the fields."

"No, not a series of workers."

"A group of workers, if you prefer."

"No, not a group, not a series."

Right, now he's playing on words, I thought.

"Do you know," he went on, "how many humans there are on Earth?"

"Between six and seven billion."

"And do you know how many genes make up each human being?"

"I don't know . . . a few thousand?"

"Slightly more than twenty thousand. And out

of the roughly six billion humans, there are not two who have the same genes!"

"Yes, each of us is unique."

"Exactly! And even if some are doing the same work, in the same place, at the same moment, you can't consider them as a group or a series, because, whatever points they have in common, there will always be more elements making them different than points in common linked to their work!"

"I understand what you mean."

"We sometimes tend to think of things by categorizing them, considering people as though they were all the same within a category, while in fact, in that field below, there are several dozen people, each with their own identity, their own history, their specific personality, their specific tastes. More than half of them live in the village. I know them. Just from the point of view of their motivation, there are differences. One does this work because he likes the contact with the water, while his neighbor has no choice. Another does it because it brings in a little more than his former job, and a fourth to help his father. The fifth likes looking after plants and seeing them grow. The sixth is there because it is the tradition in his family, and he has never thought of doing anything else.

"When we think by groups, by series, by camps, we ignore each individual's value and contribution, and we easily fall into oversimplification and generalization. We build theories that serve our beliefs. And not only are most of those theories false, but they push people to become what the theory says they are."

"I understand."

"It's a great step in life when you stop generalizing about others and consider each person individually, even if he is part of a greater whole—humanity and, even further, the universe."

I looked at the valley in the distance, which stretched for miles. Opposite us, on the other side of the void, was another hill, almost a mountain, which rose nearly as high as ours, separated by several hundred yards, forming a sort of immense canyon at the bottom of which the valley disappeared. Some clouds were lower than we were, while others were above, giving me the impression that we were floating between two worlds. A slight, persistent breeze made the heat pleasant and brought waves of fragrances, distant scents that I couldn't identify.

"Right, let's get back to what we were talking about," he said. "When you carry out your plan, since that is what you want, you will not be joining a category of people. You will just be yourself, expressing your talents in agreement with your values."

"It's true, I must remember that."

"Yes."

"You know, I have already talked a bit about

this plan to two people in my circle, and I have to say they put me off a bit."

"Why?"

"One said the profession was no doubt over-crowded and I wouldn't manage to make a place for myself just turning up like that, without qualifications or contacts. The other objected, saying that you don't start up that sort of business overnight without customers and that I had practically no chance of succeeding."

"Everybody who has a plan confronts this problem."

"Meaning?"

"When you talk about a plan with people, you get three types of reaction: the neutral ones, the encouraging ones, and the negative ones aimed at making you give up."

"That's clear . . ."

"You absolutely must steer clear of people who you feel might discourage you. At least don't tell them about your plans."

"Yes, but in a certain way, it can be useful to have people open your eyes if you're going wrong."

"For that, talk only to specialists in the area that interests you. You mustn't confide in the people who will try to discourage you just to satisfy their own psychological needs. For example, there are people who feel better when you are down and will therefore do anything to stop you from feeling better! Or others who would hate to see you fulfill your dreams because it reminds them of their lack of courage to fulfill theirs. There are also people who feel their standing is enhanced by your difficulties because it gives them the opportunity to help you. In that case, the plans that come from you cut the ground from under their feet, and they will do what they can to dissuade you. There's no point to being annoyed with them, because they do it unconsciously. But it's better not to tell them your plans. They will make you lose confidence in yourself. Do you remember we talked yesterday about the baby who is learning to walk and never loses heart, despite his repeated failures?"

"Yes."

"If he succeeds in the end, it's above all because no parent in the world doubts his baby's ability to walk, and no one in the world is going to discourage him in his attempts. Whereas, when he is an adult, countless people will try to dissuade him from fulfilling his dreams."

"That's for sure."

"That's why it's better to keep away from those people or not talk to them about your plans. Otherwise, you'll join the millions of people who don't have the life they want."

"I understand."

"On the other hand, it's very positive to have around you one or two people who believe in you."

"Who believe in me?"

"When you throw yourself into a plan that

represents a challenge, for example, when you long to change your job, there are inevitably ups and downs. You believe in it, you want it, and then, all of a sudden, you have doubts, you don't believe in it anymore, you don't feel able to do it anymore, you're afraid of change, the unknown. If you are alone at those times, there is every chance you'll give up, abandon ship. If there is someone near you who believes in you, who believes in your ability to make a success of your plan and makes you feel this when you see them, it will sweep away all your doubts, and your fears will disappear as though by magic. The confidence shown in you by that person will be contagious. It will inspire you with the strength to succeed and will give you the energy to move mountains. You are fifteen times stronger when you're not alone with your plan. But don't get me wrong: that person doesn't have to help or advise you. No, what counts above all is just that they believe in you. Moreover, you'd be surprised to know the number of famous people who have benefited from support like that at the outset."

"I'm not sure I've got someone like that . . ."

"In that case, think of someone farther away, an older relative or a childhood friend, even if you don't see them often. If you really can't find someone, you can also think of someone no longer living, who loved you when they were alive. Tell yourself, *I know that where they are, if they can see me carrying out my plan, they believe in me.* As soon as you have doubts, imagine them encouraging you because they know you will succeed."

"Then I'll choose my grandmother. I've always seen in her eyes that she was proud of me. When I got bad grades at school, my parents scolded me, but she always said, 'It doesn't matter. I know you'll get a good mark next time.'"

"That's a good example. There are also people who believe in God and get the courage to act from him. Napoleon was convinced that he had a lucky star. At most of his battles, even when they were going badly, he remained convinced that he would win, with the help of this lucky star. It motivated him enormously and gave him a strength that was often decisive."

"When I was young, I had a friend who adored her cat; she used to say that she could see in his eyes that he supported her in all circumstances. Her parents were strict and cold. When she was upset, they were not the sort to console her. So she went to see her cat, stroked him, and told him about her misfortunes. As he purred, he looked her in the eye, a deep, kindly look, and gave her back her self-confidence.

"It's very possible. An animal often has an unconditional love for its master, and that love can carry a person a long way. You know, people are beginning to do scientific research into love, and extraordinary things are being found out. In an American university, scientists growing cancer cells in a Petri dish had the idea of bringing students into their lab—in the United States, students are often used as guinea pigs. They stood them around the dish and asked them to 'send love' to the cancer cells. The students did it, and the researchers scientifically measured that the cancer cells regressed. They were incapable of explaining the phenomenon, just as they couldn't say how, concretely, the students managed to send love, but the result was there, indisputable: the cells regressed."

"That's crazy."

"Yes, love no doubt has numerous effects that we are scarcely beginning to discover. But most scientists don't like this sort of experiment, because they hate bringing to light phenomena they are not capable of explaining. Put yourself in their place: you must admit, it's frustrating.

"Now that I am near the end of my life, I find myself convinced that love is the solution to most problems human beings encounter. It may seem a simple, conventional idea, and yet practically nobody applies it, because it's often difficult to love.

"Let's say there are people you really don't feel like loving. I even get the impression sometimes some people do all they can not to be loved!

"Some are nasty because they don't love themselves. Others are annoying because they have suffered a lot and want to make the whole planet pay for it. Some have been taken in by people and believe they are protecting themselves with

an unpleasant attitude. Some have been so disappointed by others that they have closed their
hearts, saying they would not be disappointed in
the future if they no longer expected anything
from others. Others are egotistical because they
are convinced everyone is, and they think they
will be happier if they push in front of others. The
point all these people have in common is that, if
you love them, you surprise them, because they
are not expecting it. Most of them, what's more,
will refuse to believe it to start with, it seems so
abnormal. But if you persevere and demonstrate
it to them, for example by unselfish acts, it can
change their way of seeing the world and, by ex-
tension, their relation with you."

"I can accept that, but it's not easy to reach out
to people like that and have positive feelings about
them."

"It's easier if you know that another point these
people have in common is that there is still a positive intention behind each of their acts. They believe what they are doing is the best thing, even the
only thing possible. That's why, even if what they
do can be criticized, what motivates their behavior
is often understandable.

"You know, love is the best way of obtaining
a change in people. If you go toward someone
blaming him for what he did, you push him into
hardening his position and not listening to your
arguments. Feeling rejected, he will reject your

ideas. If, on the other hand, you go toward him convinced that, even if what he did or said is disastrous, he is, deep down, someone good, who had a positive intention when he did it, you make him relax and open himself to what you want to say to him. It's the only way to give him a chance to change."

"It reminds me of a story I heard on the radio, a few years ago," I said. "It was in France. A woman had been followed home by a serial rapist. She had barely opened the door when he rushed her and locked himself in the apartment with her. He was armed and, having nothing to defend herself with and not being able to shout because of the threat of his weapon, she just started talking to him. She forced the conversation, trying in vain to get him to speak. She said that this destabilized him a bit, because he was not expecting such an attitude from his victim. She carried on talking, asking questions and giving answers, hiding as best she could the terror that was taking hold of her. At one point, desperately, she had a random thought and said, 'But I don't understand why you are doing things like this when you are a good person.' She told the journalists, afterward, that her aggressor had then started to sob, and had told her, in tears, about his lousy life, while she tried to listen to him and continue to hide her terror. In the end, she got him to go away of his own accord."

"You are giving an extreme case, but it is true that people tend to behave in the way we see them, to identify with what we perceive in them. You must understand that each of us has qualities and defects; what we concentrate our attention on tends to grow, to spread. If you turn the spotlight on someone's good qualities, even if they are minute, they will be emphasized, will develop until they dominate. Hence the importance of having people close to you who believe in you."

16

"Is there another aspect of the plan that is holding you back, where you don't feel quite in agreement with yourself when you imagine yourself carrying it out?" he asked.

"Yes, there is one last point."

"What's that?"

"In my dream, I earned money, enough in any case to be able to buy myself a house with a garden, and, in fact, I'm not completely comfortable with that idea. I'm not sure whether I'm cut out to earn money, nor, deep down, whether I really want to. In short, there's something bugging me about this."

"We've gotten there!"

"Sorry?"

"I knew we'd get to this point sooner or later."

"Why?"

"Money crystallizes all our fantasies, our pro-jections, fears, hatreds, jealousies, our inferiority complexes, our superiority complexes, and many other things as well. It would have been astonishing if we didn't have to tackle it together."

"I didn't know such a little word hid so many things!"

"Come on, tell me everything. What is your worry about money?"

He kept his kindly tone, but I could make out an added tone of amusement, as if he had already explored the question so much that he was absolutely not expecting to be surprised by anything I was about to lay before him, whatever it was.

"Let's say I'm of two minds on the question. It's as if part of me wanted to earn money and another part didn't, thought it was contaminated."

"So the question is how to reconcile the two parts of you, isn't it?"

"It's amusing to put it like that, but you could say that, it's true."

"So, to start with, tell me what the part of you that wants to earn money wants."

"I think money might give me a certain freedom. I feel that the richer you are, the less you depend on others. As a result, you become free with your time, with your activities—you don't owe anyone explanations."

"There's some truth in that. What else?"

"Well, I want to make sure I have a certain material comfort. I'm foolish enough to think that it is easier to be happy in a lovely, peaceful house than in a run-down studio apartment in a noisy, polluted neighborhood."

"There is no harm in seeking material comfort, and it is true that it can make things easier. To be more precise, material comfort doesn't bring happiness; on the other hand, its absence can sometimes spoil happiness."

"That seems obvious to me."

"Yet I must emphasize that material things cannot bring happiness. Many people agree with that idea, and sometimes even assert it loud and clear, and yet, deep down, unconsciously, they still believe it would make them happy. So they denounce the behavior of those who flaunt their wealth, but this denunciation is in reality tainted with jealousy because a part of them is envious and thinks the wealthy are happier than they are. This belief is widespread, including among those who state the contrary."

"Yes, that's possible."

I recalled one of my friends, who so violently criticized the rich and those who only thought of material things that it seemed fishy. Her lack of indifference toward them no doubt betrayed a particular echo that their money produced in her and which was, perhaps, not harmless.

"In fact, it's the belief itself that makes you unhappy, since it impels people to an endless race. You desire an object, a car, an article of clothing, or whatever, and you begin to believe that possessing that object will satisfy you. You desire it, you want it, and, in the end, if you get it, you forget it very quickly and set your sights on something else that will, of course, satisfy you if you get it. There is no end to this quest. People don't realize that if they drove a Ferrari, lived in a Beverly Hills apartment, and traveled by private jet, they would be convinced that it was the yacht they didn't yet own that would make them happy. Of course, people who are nowhere near being able to drive a Ferrari are annoyed and tell themselves they would be happy just to be a bit richer than they are. They're not asking for a mansion in Beverly Hills, just a slightly larger apartment, and they are convinced that would be enough and they wouldn't want anything else afterward. That's where they're wrong. Whatever the material level you aspire to, you desire more when you reach it. It's really an endless race."

His words resonated with me, because they reminded me of childhood Christmases. I would be all excited preparing my letter to Santa Claus, preparing the list of toys I wanted. For weeks I would think about it, impatiently waiting for the day when I would finally possess them. My excitement reached a peak on Christmas Eve: I couldn't take my eyes off the tree, underneath which I already imagined my happiness the next day. When I went to bed, the night ahead seemed interminable, and I was grateful to see the time on my alarm clock at first light. The big day had finally arrived! When I opened the living room door and saw the multicolored parcels under the lit-up tree, I was filled with an intense joy. I unwrapped everything, breathless with excitement, then spent most of the day playing with what I had been given, making sure I avoided the long family meal, leaving the adults to their boring conversations. But I remember that, as evening came, as the sun went down, my joy progressively dried up. Already, my new toys no longer generated the same rush of pleasure. I would even find myself wishing for the excitement of the day before. I would have liked to relive that. I remember telling myself one year that my dreams of toys made me happier than the toys themselves. Waiting was more pleasurable than the outcome.

I told the sage about this, who said with a smile, "The parents' biggest lie to their children is not about Santa Claus. It's the tacit promise that his presents will make them happy."

I again looked at the workers in the valley and wondered if their traditions also led them, once a year, to try to bring happiness to their children by showering them with material presents.

"You have told me," he went on, "what motivates the part of you that wants to earn money. Tell me now about the part of you that rejects the idea."

"I think money in itself disgusts me a little. I sometimes feel that it is all that counts in this world, that money becomes the center of people's concerns."

"Things are going off course a little, it's true, and it's a pity because money is a fine invention."

"Why do you say that?"

"We often forget that, originally, money was no more than a means of making exchanges between human beings easier: exchanges of goods, but also of skills, services, advice. Before money, there was barter. A person who needed something was forced to find someone who was interested in what he had to offer in exchange. Not easy. The creation of money allowed the evaluation of each object, each service, and the money collected by the seller then gave him the chance to acquire other goods and services. There is no harm in that. In a way, you could even say that the more money circulates, the more exchanges there are between human beings, and the better it is."

"Looked at like that, it's amazing!"

"That's how it should be: offering up what you are capable of—the fruit of your labor, your skills—and obtaining in exchange the wherewithal to acquire what others can do and you can't. Besides, money is not something that should be accumulated, but used. If everyone started from this principle, unemployment would not exist, because there are no limits to the services that human beings can render each other. It would be enough to favor people's creativity and encourage them to realize their ideas."

"So why has money become something dirty nowadays?"

"To understand that, you must first grasp two elements: how money is earned and how it is spent. Money is healthy if it comes from the employment of our skills, giving the best of ourselves. In this way, it gives real satisfaction to the person who earns it. But if it is obtained by abusing others—for example, your customers or your co-workers—then it generates what we could call symbolically a negative energy; shamans call it *hucha*. And this hucha pulls everyone down, pollutes minds and, in the end, makes both despoiled and despoiler unhappy. The despoiler may well feel that he has won something, but he builds up in himself the hucha that will increasingly prevent him from being happy. You can see it in the face when people get old, no matter the wealth accumulated. While the man who earns money by giving the best of himself and respecting others can blossom as he gets rich."

I couldn't stop myself from thinking of *The Picture of Dorian Gray*, Oscar Wilde's incredible novel about a malevolent man whose malevolent acts are written on the face of his portrait instead of his own face. Over time, the portrait is marked more and more, until it becomes hideous.

"You said too that the way you spend money is important."

"Yes, if you use the money you earn to give others the possibility of expressing their talents, their skills, by calling on their services, then money produces positive energy. On the other hand, if you satisfy yourself with accumulating material goods, then life is emptied of its meaning. You dry out little by little. Look around you: people who have spent their lives accumulating without giving anything are disconnected from others. They no longer have any real human relationships. They are no longer capable of taking a sincere interest in a person, or of loving. And, believe me, when you reach that stage, you're not happy!"

"It's strange, when I think of it: I'm at the other end of the world, I meet a spiritual master, and we talk about money!"

"In fact, we're not really talking about money."

"What do you mean?"

"We're talking about the limits you set in life. Money is only a metaphor for your potential."

I was swinging my legs over the void and looking at the immense space open before me. The slight warm breeze continued to tease my nostrils with aerial scents and murmur its secrets in my ears.

"In the end, perhaps I earn enough money today, and it's not necessary to have more. But, tell me, since you are so comfortable about money, how come you're not filthy rich?"

He smiled, before answering, "Because I don't need it."

"So, why are you helping me to be more comfortable about earning money?"

"Because perhaps you need to earn some before you can detach yourself from it."

"And suppose I were already detached?"

After a short silence, he said, "It's not detachment; it's renunciation."

His words echoed in me, and the impression of the echo of his voice carried on vibrating.

I had to admit that, once again, he was right.

"In Hindu philosophy," he went on, "it is thought that earning money is a valuable goal, and it corresponds to one of the phases of life. You must just avoid getting stuck in it, and then know how to evolve toward something else to make a success of your life."

"What's a successful life?" I asked, feeling a little naive.

"A successful life is a life that you have led in accordance with your wishes, giving the best of yourself in what you do, staying in harmony with who you are, and, if possible, a life that has given us the chance to go beyond yourself, to devote yourself to something other than yourself and to bring something to mankind, even very humbly, even if it's tiny. A little bird's feather thrown to the wind. A smile for other people."

"That presupposes you know your wishes."

"Yes."

"And how can you know if you are acting in accord with your values?"

"By being on the lookout for what you feel. If what you are doing does not respect your values, you will experience a certain discomfort, a slight malaise, or a feeling of guilt. It's a sign that you must ask yourself if your actions are in conflict with what is important for you. You can also ask yourself, at the end of a day, if you are proud of what you have accomplished. It's very important: we can't develop as human beings, or even simply stay in good health, when we are doing things that violate our values."

"It's funny that you should make a link with health, because I remember when I was a student, I did a summer job as a telemarketing representative for an insurance company. I had to call people to advise them to take out a certain policy. The company knew that three-quarters of the people contacted already had this coverage without knowing it, among the services included with their credit card. But we were absolutely not to mention this, and we were to offer the coverage to everyone. That summer, for the first time in my life, I had a dreadful attack of eczema. The doctor never managed to identify the cause of it, and the prescribed medicine changed nothing; I stopped taking it. The eczema continued to develop, and in the end, I stopped the work because I was ashamed to turn up at the office in that state. A week after I quit, it had all gone."

"You can't be sure, of course, but it was perhaps a message from your body that you were acting in conflict with your values of respect for others, trust, and honesty."

"It's true they are fundamental values for me."

"I'm sure."

"You were saying also that you must give of your best in what you are doing?"

"Yes, it's one of the keys to happiness. You know, human beings delight in sloppiness, but bloom when making demands on themselves. It's really by being focused on what we are doing to succeed in applying our skills and abilities, and by taking up new challenges each time, that we feel happy. It's true for everyone, whatever the job or skill level, and our happiness is increased if our work brings something to others, even indirectly, even modestly."

At that precise moment, my memory took me back four years. I was in Morocco, in Marrakesh. I was strolling around Djemaa el-Fna square at the end of the day. Night plunged the square into an enchanting atmosphere. Charcoal fires with meat grilling on them were crackling at the numerous restaurants. The flames cast their glow on the crowd of passersby, fleetingly lighting up faces and making huge dancing shadows. The smell of grilled merguez competed with the smell of steaming couscous. Street peddlers were everywhere. Some offered leather goods barely out of the nearby tanneries, which still had an acidic, aggressive smell. Others displayed great big engraved brass trays that reflected the light from the fires, making golden flashes spring from faces, turbans, and djellabas. The noise of voices mixed with the throbbing sounds of drums and the melodies of the snake charmers' flutes. I was walking, eyes wide, enchanted by the incredible atmosphere, my senses saturated with perfumes, images, and sounds, when I was stopped by a little man of about 50, slim, all smiles, his face furrowed by the southern sun. He sat on a box placed directly on the beaten earth, with a steaming restaurant on one side of him and a pottery dealer on the other. I smiled back and looked at the chair he was pointing to for me to sit down. That's when I understood his trade. Shoe shiner. My smile froze, and I stiffened imperceptibly. I had never felt at ease with trades that required those practicing them to perform thankless tasks. Shoe shiner was perhaps the one I accepted with the greatest difficulty, because the worker operates in the presence of his customer, in front of him, on him. Even the respective postures embarrassed me: the customer sat on a high chair, dominating the situation; the shoe shiner below, squatting, seated, or kneeling. I had never gotten used this kind of service.

The man renewed his invitation and gently insisted, still giving me his beaming smile. As a Westerner, I represented, no doubt, the ideal customer. But precisely my position as a foreigner accentuated my unease: I didn't want to give his compatriots the sight of a Westerner having his shoes cleaned by one of them. A nasty colonialist cliché. I don't know if he saw my unease or interpreted it as hesitation. Perhaps simply my absence of indifference to his proposition gave him the hope of convincing me. He got up, still smiling, and came over to me. I didn't have time to express a refusal: he was already upon me, examining my shabby shoes while formulating his diagnosis and the promise to rejuvenate them.

No doubt my problem with turning down other people's requests explains how I came to be, in spite of myself, sitting in the chair I was looking at a moment before with repugnance. I didn't dare look at the people around me for fear of encountering accusing eyes. He was already busy with my shoes. Grabbing half a lemon, he was energetically rubbing the shabby leather with it. In the state I was in, I shouldn't have been surprised by anything. I don't think I would have been more surprised if he had rubbed a banana into my shoes. He applied himself enthusiastically. Sure of himself, he was in control of his movements, alternating the lemon and different types of brush. Afar, the snake charmer's flute kept up its lament without stopping.

I was beginning to unstiffen a little. We exchanged a few sentences, but he remained very focused on what he was doing, still displaying his ineffable smile. He applied a sort of blackish cream with an old rag, massaging the leather to work it in. Then he started to make it shine with a nimble little brush, and, as my shoes came back to life, his smile grew wider, revealing dazzling teeth whose whiteness contrasted with his brown skin. Once my shoes were as smooth and shiny as when they were new, his eyes shone with pride. I had completely forgotten my initial embarrassment. His joy was infectious, and I suddenly felt very close to this man who was a stranger 15 minutes before. I felt a real spurt of sympathy for him, like a wave of friendship.

He named an honest price which I willingly handed over, and, in the heat of the moment, he insisted on offering me mint tea in a little metal cup, sharing his joy by prolonging the relationship. I suddenly became aware of something that then seemed obvious, painfully obvious: this man was happier than I, who had a respected profession and who, despite my modest means, was no doubt a thousand times richer than he was. This man radiated happiness through every pore of his body, and his happiness shone around him.

Just remembering this scene, I had tears in my eyes.

"Why did you talk of the usefulness of having challenges to meet so that we can feel happy by using our skills?" I asked.

"Because a challenge stimulates our concentration, pushes us to give our best in what we do and draw real satisfaction from it afterward. It's a precondition for blossoming in what we do."

"You said as well that a life is successful when

you accomplish things in harmony with what you are. But how do you know if that's the case?"

"Imagine you are going to die tonight, and all this past week, you have known this would happen. What would you have done differently during your last week?"

"Now, there's a question!"

"Yes."

"Let's say that this last week was a bit special, given our meeting. There is not much I would change."

"Right, take the week before your journey to Bali."

"Well . . . let's say . . . er . . . let's see . . ."

In my mind I tried to rerun the film of the week in question. I tried hard to visualize hour by hour what I had done, and, for each of my actions, I asked myself if I would really have done it, knowing that I was going to die at the end of the week. It took me several minutes to reply: "Roughly, there are about thirty percent of my actions I would have kept."

"You're telling me that you would have given up doing seventy percent of what you did, if you had known you were going to die?"

"Well, yes."

"It's too much, much too much. It's normal to carry out certain meaningless tasks, but not to that extent. In fact, you ought to be able to reverse the proportion: be able to assert that, knowing you are about to die, you would continue to carry out seventy percent of what you normally do. It would be a sign that your actions are in harmony with who you are."

"I see."

"And you will observe that it doesn't relate to the difficulty of the tasks, simply the meaning they have for you."

"Fine, I agree with all this in the absolute, but in practice it's not always possible to do what you want to do."

"You always have the choice."

"No, if I only did what was in accord with myself, I would lose my job—"

"So you have the choice of keeping or losing your job."

"But in that case, I would have to find another, perhaps less well paid. I might not be able to pay my rent anymore!"

"Then you would have the choice of keeping that apartment or taking another, cheaper one, perhaps farther from your work."

"My family and friends would be disappointed if I moved away."

"So, you would have the choice of satisfying them or disappointing them."

"Looked at like that . . ."

"It's just to say that the choice is yours. At certain moments in life, you don't necessarily have a lot of choices, and they are painful perhaps, but they exist. In the end, you alone decide how you live: you always have the choice, and it's good to keep that in mind."

"I sometimes have the impression that it's others who decide for me."

"Then you are choosing to let them decide for you."

"All the same, I think there are people who have more choices than others."

"The more you go through life, the more you get rid of the beliefs that limit you, the more choice you have. And choice is freedom."

I looked at the immense space in front of me, the dizzying space stopped by nothing, and I started dreaming of freedom. My eyes fixed on the horizon, deeply inhaling this intoxicating air, with its perfume of infinity.

"You know," he went on, "you can't be happy if you see yourself as the victim of events or others' desires. It is important to understand that it's always you who decides, whatever it is. Even if you are the lowest of the low at work, you are the director of your life. You're in command of the controls. You're the master of your destiny."

"Yes."

"And you mustn't be afraid: you will discover that it's precisely when you allow yourself to choose actions that are in harmony with yourself, that respect your values and express your abilities, that you become precious to others. Doors open of their own accord. Everything becomes easier, and you no longer need to struggle to move forward."

We remained silent for a long while. Then he got up, and I broke the silence.

"I phoned about my plane ticket. I can't change it without paying an expensive surcharge. You had planned to tell me today if there were still important things left for me to discover that would make it necessary for us to meet tomorrow."

"I think there is one major apprenticeship left."

"And tomorrow you're still not available in the morning?"

"No."

"Forgive me insisting, but can you really not free yourself so I can make my afternoon flight?"

"No."

I was really out of luck. I was faced with a tough choice: should I abandon the final one of these meetings which enthralled me and were awaking me to myself or pay a scandalously high price to put off my return?

"What would you do in my place? Would you change flights?"

"It's for you to choose," he said, a satisfied smile playing on his lips, his kindly gaze looking down into my questioning eyes.

Infinity was reflected in his pupils.

He walked away toward the campan, with his slow, serene gait, and I lost sight of him when he entered the thicket of bamboo.

Six hundred dollars! It amounted almost to buying a second return ticket! Difficult to accept . . . It would weigh heavily on my bank account, increasing the spectacular overdraft it must be showing already. Relations with my bank manager would be affected for a while. Not to mention that taking the plane on Sunday would ensure that I'd arrive home tired, only a few hours before starting work again. Not a very enjoyable prospect. At the same time, it wasn't every day that you had the chance to meet a man like Master Samtyang. But it made for an expensive session! Really, I didn't know what to do anymore. Each option seemed painful, and I couldn't decide.

I was in the car and nearing Ubud. I had to decide now because, to change my ticket, I had to stop at the travel agency in Kuta before it closed. I was coming up to the place where I would have to choose my route.

I tried to weigh the pros and cons. To no avail. There were wins and losses in both situations. An impossible choice! I wasn't going to flip a coin, though; there wouldn't exactly be anything illustrious about that: after five days of personal development, in all conscience I ought to be capable of reaching a decision!

In the end, my conscience told me that I would get over a hectic start of term and that I would of course find a way of paying off my overdraft one day. In six months or a year, I would have forgotten this difficult moment. Whereas I could no doubt profit for a long time from what the healer was going to teach me, all my life perhaps. I arrived at the crossroads and headed south, toward Kuta. As Oscar Wilde said, "the only thing one never regrets are one's mistakes"!

I remembered what the president of Mexico said at a time when his country was running up colossal debts. A journalist asked him if he was losing sleep. He said an overdraft of a thousand dollars stopped you from sleeping at night, but, for an overdraft of a hundred billion dollars, it was your banker who lost sleep. I concluded that my debts were no doubt still very inadequate.

It took me nearly an hour to reach Kuta. I didn't like the place. For me, Kuta was not Bali. It was where the greatest concentration of tourists was, particularly Australian surfers. After dark, the town was transformed into a gigantic nightclub. It was impossible to walk a yard without being accosted by a Javanese offering you drugs or a prostitute. In the '70s, Kuta was part of the hippies' must-see circuit of the three *K*'s: Kuta, Kathmandu, Kabul. In 2002, Kuta, symbol of Western excess, was chosen by al-Qaida for one of its bloodiest bomb attacks.

The journey took longer than expected, and I arrived at the end of the afternoon. The travel agency was closing its doors in ten minutes. I turned up the narrow one-way street at top speed, and by a miracle, I spotted a parking place just outside the office. I went past the space so I could back in—then noticed that the car behind hadn't stopped, even though my intention to park was obvious. Not only had I put my signal on in advance, but I had also pulled over slightly to the side of the road to show I intended to park there. No, he had to follow me, preventing me from backing up. For a moment I stayed there, jutting out with my signal on, in order to get him to understand my maneuver, but it was no good.

I lowered my window, put my head out, and asked him to reverse a bit so I could park. No other car was following him; it would have been easy. It was clear he understood me, especially as I was reinforcing my words with explicit gestures. To no avail. A Westerner, in his late 50s, he had a crimson face, a symptom common to fair-skinned people who have been in the sun too much and to alcoholics. In his case, I opted readily for the second explanation. He had the stubborn look of those who have no flexibility of mind and never want to let things drop. His posture gave off an incredible sense of inertia. He seemed as heavy as his car, rooted to the spot. I repeated my gestures and my words. Nothing. Obtuse face, rigid shoulders, fixed arms, big hands clenched on the wheel: his whole body expressed his desire not to give in. Because giving in was clearly the way he interpreted the action of backing up two yards. It seemed obvious to me: in his life, his relations with others must be governed by force, and no doubt he must believe that responding to someone's request amounted to giving ground, to showing weakness. Yes, that was it! He must have a belief along the lines of "never let anyone get the better of you, never budge an inch."

In other circumstances, I would have found him funny, even if those around him probably didn't think he was a barrel of laughs. But the travel agency was closing in five minutes. I had no choice; I had to get that place—there was no time to find another. Then I heard the sage's words in my head: you always have a choice. Suddenly I said to myself that I could fight inertia with inertia. I switched off, put the hand brake on, and left the car in the middle of the road, blocking the street. I rushed into the travel agent's office and held out my ticket to the employee, who had already

149

started switching off the lights. The pattering of his computer keyboard was soon drowned out by a continuous car horn. I handed over my credit card, slightly anxious, praying that the transaction wouldn't be refused. The operation took a little time, which seemed ominous, but, in the end, the system accepted the card—I had become a bit poorer.

My wallet lighter, a new plane ticket in my pocket, I went back to my car. The driver was beside himself with rage. He kept his hand on the horn and only took it off to release a torrent of insults. I gave him my nicest smile, which only doubled his anger. I pulled away, and he followed so closely that I thought he was going to push me. It was really ridiculous. Then I understood fully the idea of choice talked about by the healer. What was striking about this driver was the absence of choice of behaviors dictated by his personality. He could neither reverse nor negotiate nor be patient. All he could do was force his way through. This man was not free. On the contrary, he was in the grip of his beliefs. It was obvious. A fortnight before, I would just have said, "What an idiot!" Today, I could see that intelligence probably had nothing to do with his extraordinary attitude.

I was astonished at my new understanding of behaviors that I used to reject with, no doubt, a certain intolerance. Carried along by this new understanding and compassion, it made me want to observe and listen to people more, to try to discover the beliefs that were perhaps the origin of their attitudes.

I went to the seafront and sat at a table on the terrace of a handsome café and ice cream parlor. I have always been in the habit of spending to console myself for my money troubles.

I ordered a chocolate-avocado cocktail, a surprising but absolutely delicious mixture, and settled into the comfortable teak armchair facing the sea. The wind must have been blowing hard, because the waves were particularly high. The late-afternoon sun was flooding the shore with its warm orange light, so flattering to the houses, as well as people's faces. The beach was emptying itself onto my café terrace, which was becoming gradually livelier. It was good to be alone without really being alone, to enjoy the growing ambiance without having to contribute to making it.

At the next table, two young people were talking. She was delicate and pretty, with chestnut hair and blue eyes, a slightly sulky look; he was not very tall but fairly beefy, with a thick neck and dark brown hair cut short. She called him Dick. She was telling him about the shadow play she had been to the night before, which had visibly fascinated her. He was listening to her attentively, but it seemed clear to me that a few shadows, however artistically done, wouldn't have been enough to move him.

Perhaps, nonetheless, he was moved by the sensitivity she was voicing. I felt they were not a couple, but she had feelings for him she had not yet made obvious. He called her Doris, and I was unable to guess what he felt for her. Dick was one of those men so virile that you don't know if emotions and feelings are part of their basic equipment. I amused myself imagining him as a caveman dragging his mate off by the hair to his bed.

At a table next to theirs, a teenage surfer, half pimply youth, half pretentious dolt, was drinking a whiskey and Coke. He was eyeing Doris attentively, but I had the impression that any girl would have awoken the same interest in him. He and I had one thing in common: we were not missing one word of the conversation next to us.

After a quarter of an hour, Dick and Doris were joined by a girl their age, who was accompanied by someone they apparently didn't know.

"Hi, Kate!" said Dick.

"Hi, Dick. Hi, Doris."

I immediately felt Doris clam up just slightly. She seemed put out. It was clear she didn't like Kate. What was going on between them?

A brunette with a provocative air, Kate was sexy rather than really beautiful. Rather high heels for the seaside, a miniskirt and breasts on display. She didn't have much in the way of breasts, but Saint Wonderbra had been by, and the effect was satisfying. Anyhow, at the neighboring table, the teenage surfer couldn't take his eyes off her cleavage. She smiled as she talked, working on the super-cool attitude of the girl at ease with her looks, at ease with her body.

"Sorry I'm late. I got changed after the beach, and I couldn't find my things. Impossible to find my panties."

It was obvious the young surfer intended to learn whether she had found them or not: his eyes had gone down from the cleavage to the miniskirt, which he was now staring at intently, waiting for the moment that would reveal the answer. Doris's exasperation went up a notch. Kate was satisfied.

"Let me introduce Jenz. We met on the beach. You wouldn't believe it, like, we both smoke Marlboro menthol lights. It's crazy!" said Kate.

Very thin and hollow-cheeked, with an affable smile, Jenz introduced himself as coming from "a little European country," Denmark as it turned out. The size of his bald patch had led him to shave his head completely, a clever way of hiding it from others. But, on the other hand, he was sporting a dense, dark blond beard. You got the feeling he was trying to compensate with his beard for the lack of hair on the top of his head. His voice was soft, to the extent that you had to listen hard to hear it. He replied to the others' questions with a humility bordering on self-deprecation, like he was excusing himself for saying sorry for being a nuisance. Dick frowned slightly as he looked at him, as though he was wondering what type of animal this was. For him, it was obviously not natural that a man should be so retiring. Jenz was trying so hard not to offend that he was transparent. After five minutes, everyone had forgotten he was there. He no longer existed.

What could push someone to act like that? Would it be something like "they'll leave me alone if I make myself small"? At any rate, I was sure that Dick had the opposite belief, along the lines of "they'll respect me if I'm strong!"

Jenz was looking lovingly at Kate, who hadn't once looked at him since introducing him to the others. She was completely ignoring him. Why had she brought him into the group? For the pleasure of being seen with a vacuous admirer who demonstrated her powers of seduction? To make Dick react? It did seem to me that she was doing her best to grab his attention. Doris must feel it as well, because her exasperated gaze at times threw out sparks of hatred.

The barman was taking their orders.

"A blue lagoon," Kate asked.

"Sparkling water," said Doris.

"What are you having?" Dick asked Jenz.

"Whatever."

"Make up your mind!"

"Right, I'll have the same as you."

"Two beers," Dick ordered.

Dick had had a good day. "The waves were

awesome today, man, it rocked. At last, a kickass day," he said.

"It was lovely to see the elements unleashed," added Doris.

"You're right," Jenz slipped in.

"Oh, no! It was a drag today," said Kate. "There were two guys who wouldn't stop trying to pick me up. I was pissed—they wouldn't back off."

"Just go surfing," replied Dick. "In the water, guys just look at the waves."

"Oh, no! Not surfing. You fall all the time, and I might hurt my breasts if I did a belly flop."

On the next table, the young surfer's eyes went back up from the miniskirt to the cleavage.

Doris had decided not to fight. Hypersensitive, she was one of those people who want to be loved for themselves, as they are, to the point that she had developed the belief that if she tried hard to please, she wouldn't be loved for who she was, but only for what she had done.

"Do you know why a man ejaculates in spurts?" Kate called out, creating a silence that was half embarrassed, half expectant.

Dick obviously appreciated the joke and was waiting for the punch line. Doris's face displayed her contempt for vulgarity. Jenz was smiling ingratiatingly.

"Because a woman swallows in sips," she went on, holding Dick's gaze.

Jenz laughed stupidly, Dick coarsely. Doris was appalled.

The young surfer couldn't believe it. He hadn't known girls like that existed. Openmouthed, he kept his eyes riveted on her, staring hungrily. He must have been thinking she was an incredible lay. I was decidedly less sure about that: in my opinion, she was much more interested in the effect she had on men than in men themselves.

What could make a girl act provocatively to the point of telling obscene stories in public? What was she after? What must she believe about herself and others? No doubt she had a visceral desire to seduce, to arouse sexual desire in the other. I was beginning to see a couple of possible beliefs: "I exist if I seduce" or "I have value if I succeed in attracting men." At any rate, I felt that her aggressive seduction wasn't really a choice, that it spoke to a need to which she was a slave.

I had started listening to people to have fun trying to guess their beliefs, but the more I discovered, the sadder I was to observe that human beings are not free. This absence of freedom didn't come from some terrible dictator, but just from what each person believed about themselves, others, and the world.

On the sand, parents were organizing beach games for their children. I observed them for a moment and was surprised to hear them pushing their offspring to compete with the others. It wasn't enough for them to be successful in their activities; they had to beat their little playmates, be *better* than them. What could the parents believe? That you are only of value when you beat others? That a result is only valid if it is better than the neighbor's? I felt rather that the only valid competition was with yourself. Surpassing yourself rather than others. The sage had told me that you couldn't judge a belief, merely take an interest in its effects. What could they be in such a case? A stimulus? Certainly. Motivation to progress. But what were the effects on your relationship to others? Can you experience friendship or love when you are used to comparing yourself to others? And what do you feel with other people? Do you swing between feelings of superiority and inferiority? Or pity and jealousy? These parents had no idea what they were creating in their children, something that was going to lastingly determine their lives in society. Their motives, their behaviors, their emotions would be marked in this way by a few beliefs inculcated at an age when you absorb models offered by the outside world.

Besides, how had these parents developed these beliefs? Did they get them from their own parents, or had they been faced with competitive people and, having been humiliated, now wanted their children to be in the position of the people who had dominated them? In that case, where was their choice?

Another nearby table had been occupied. A know-it-all was talking with a lady who was skillfully letting him think that she admired his erudition, whereas, obviously, she was hiding her boredom. On each subject, he tried hard to display his knowledge. He even picked up on her mistakes when she spoke, which was rare, given what little latitude he allowed her. I wondered which of them to pity more in this situation; he seemed so desperate to show what he knew. Perhaps he believed he didn't exist except in his knowledge? Perhaps he was afraid to be thought of as an idiot or an ignoramus? Or perhaps he thought he couldn't be loved by someone who didn't perceive his erudition, so he felt obliged to demonstrate it to her?

The point all these people had in common was how little freedom they seemed to enjoy. They were grappling with their beliefs, and these beliefs restricted their choices by dictating their behavior. I was becoming more and more conscious of this. All I had to do now was listen to and observe strangers for a few moments to see the beliefs that underpinned their attitude. I was David Vincent in *The Invaders*. He could identify the aliens by their stiff little fingers; they were everywhere and had invaded the planet. My planet had been invaded by people's beliefs.

I GOT BACK in my car, not sorry to leave Kuta, with its bars and overrated atmosphere, and arrived at my bungalow in the black, hot night. My ritual swim was heavenly.

Saturday morning seemed interminable. I spent it on the beach under the shade of a palm tree, observing the occasional comings and goings of the fishermen. I awaited the afternoon with impatience. I wondered what the famous "major apprenticeship" that the sage was keeping for our last meeting could be. Besides, I found it difficult to believe that this was our last meeting. I had gotten used to them, and each one had so awakened me to myself that it was difficult to accept that the cycle was going to end.

Why had I decided to meet the healer that first time? What wild stroke of luck had led me to hear of him and to come and see him when, on the face of it, I had no need of him? Life is weird; sometimes tiny decisions have incredible consequences. And years later, you wonder how it would have turned out if you hadn't, at the time, made that tiny decision but another one. How many times, in the thousands of little crossings of my life, had I opted for the banal path, while the other would have turned out to be marvelous?

I had a quick, early breakfast. I wanted to see the sage at the very beginning of the afternoon so we would have a long period of time together. My motives for this were heightened by the fact that it was our last meeting—but also, I had to recognize, because of what it had cost me. Fate had decreed that I was to arrive within sight of his campan at the very time the plane I should have been on was taking off.

The garden was as I had seen it the first time, simple and beautiful, with its delicately perfumed flowers from the other side of the world. I walked forward and saw no one at first. The campan where he usually met me was empty. All was quiet. Perhaps I had come too early. I walked all around it: not a living soul. I sat down on a wall near the entrance and waited. The silence of the place was broken only by the odd rustling of leaves and the familiar cry of the gecko no doubt hidden in the rafters. Such calm was favorable to serenity and, for the first time, I told myself that I wasn't made for living in a city. Twenty minutes went by before at last the young woman with the chignon appeared. I went up to her, and she anticipated my question.

"Master Samtyang isn't available today," she said.

"Yes he is. I know he was busy this morning, but he planned to see me this afternoon. Perhaps he didn't inform you. Can you tell him I've arrived?"

"But he isn't here."

"Okay, he's probably late. In that case, I'll go and wait for him in the campan," I said, making as though to move.

"No, he won't come back today. He said as he left that I would see him tomorrow."

"You must be mistaken," I asserted. "I assure you that I have an appointment with him. It's impossible that he forgot."

"He didn't forget, but he isn't here, and you won't see him." She expressed herself with the same naturalness as usual, taking no notice of my dismay.

"What do you mean, he hasn't forgotten?" I said, feeling anger mounting in me.

"He did indeed tell me you'd come this afternoon."

"What's going on?" I exploded. "I changed my airline ticket at his request, purposely to meet him. I must see him. Where is he?"

"I don't know."

The situation was beyond belief. I had the impression of being in a bad dream.

"Did he ask you to tell me anything?"

"Didn't you see the message he left you?"

"Where?"

"In the campan."

I ran there, disgusted by the turn of events. Why play this trick on me? He knew what the change of ticket cost me. What excuse would he have?

The message was sitting on the camphor wood box. A little yellowy piece of paper, folded in four. I leapt on it and unfolded it. I recognized his light, sinuous writing:

The disappointment, dismay, or perhaps even anger that you must feel as you start to read this message will accompany your transition to a new dimension of your being, one in which you no longer need me to continue your evolution.

By making the decision to come today, you have achieved a major apprenticeship for yourself. You developed an ability that was cruelly lacking in you until now: the ability to make a choice that costs you something and therefore to give something up—in other words, to make sacrifices in order to advance on your path. Thus the final obstacle to your self-fulfillment has been broken into pieces. Now you have at your disposal a strength that will accompany you all your life. The path that leads to happiness sometimes requires you to renounce the easy way, to follow the demands of its will in the depths of yourself.

Have a good journey.

Samtyang

I remained silent for a long while as I progressed from anger to stupefaction, from stupefaction to doubt, from doubt to understanding, from understanding to acceptance, from acceptance to gratitude, from gratitude to admiration.

This man had had the guts to impose a test on me, knowing that I would be angry with him and might even not forgive him. He had done it because it wasn't enough to understand, nor even to share an idea, in order to change. You had to experience something intense, involving you personally—that was what he had given me.

By leaving, he had forgone my farewell, my thanks, and my gratitude for all he had given me. And, by that act, he demonstrated what he had just taught me, amplifying the strength of his message. It was high art.

I remained alone a long while, filling myself for the last time with the atmosphere of this place, so special, loaded with meaning, then my hands went to my neck and unclasped the chain with the cross that I was wearing. I carefully took it and put it in the little box on the shelf.

I SET BACK off and, after a short stop in a village to fill my bag with provisions, headed due north at top speed. Half an hour later, I stopped, tightened my shoelaces, put on my bag, and set off on the path. After a few minutes walking, I already strongly felt the heat, and the sweat was beginning to form on my forehead. I looked up, my hand in front of my eyes to protect them from the sun. Dominating me with all its height, like a magnificent giant, immobile and immutable, was Mount Skouwo.

The climb took me nearly four hours. Four hours of effort and, at certain moments, of suffering. The climb was sometimes steep, and I got out of breath. Sometimes the path went along the side of the mountain at the same height, and I recharged my batteries, breathing in the air perfumed with tropical bushes whose names I didn't know. The higher I went, the more impressive the view was.

I reached the summit exhausted, emptied of energy but filled with an intense satisfaction. I had succeeded in surmounting my laziness, in mobilizing my courage and strength, in following all the way through on my decision. Now I felt all-powerful and stood on Mount Skouwo like a captain at the bow of his ship, overlooking miles of fields, rice paddies, and forests, the wind whistling in my ears, intoxicating me with a perfume of adventure.

A new life was beginning for me, and, henceforth, it would be *my* life, the fruit of my decisions, of my choices, of my will. Farewell to doubts, hesitations, and the fear of being judged, of not being able, of not being loved. I would live each moment consciously, in accord with myself and with my values. I would remain an altruist, but remember that the first present to give others is my balance. I would accept difficulties as challenges to be faced, presents given to me to develop. I would no longer be the victim of events, but an actor in a play whose rules were uncovered little by little, and whose final purpose would always keep a measure of mystery.

The way down was fast, and I made a detour to sit beside the lake at the foot of the mountain, over which reigned the temple of the goddess of the waters. A magical place, of unbelievable beauty. The setting sun soon disappeared, and the scene became magical. A vast stretch of water dominated by the gigantic shadow of Mount Skouwo. No habitation in sight. Not a living soul. Absolute silence. And the black temple with its pagoda roof stood out like a Chinese shadow on the white reflection of the clouds, on the surface of the lake. I remained there for a long while, drinking in the serenity of the place, filling myself with calm and beauty.

I drove back to my bungalow in the dark, concentrating on the road to avoid the numerous Balinese cars driving with no lights on. I arrived at once tired and light. I went to the water's edge. The ascending moon bathed my beach in a restful atmosphere. Nobody. The fishermen's families had long since left the spot.

I got completely undressed and entered the warm water naked. I swam in silence, relaxed and free, feeling the water gliding over my body. I had the impression of swaying with the slow movement of the waves and merging with the ocean. I took a deep breath and went down into the water, diving toward the bottom. I seized a stone resting on the sand. Its weight allowed me to float, neither drawn to the surface nor dragged to the bottom. I curled myself up, drawing my knees up to my chest, keeping the stone in my arms. I stayed like that a long while, weightless, immersed in that warm, gentle water, feeling the muffled, dull sound of the waves on the surface as regular, calming pulsations.

I WOKE UP on the sand after the sun was up. I remembered falling asleep on the beach—I had my clothes on, though, a sign that I hadn't been carried by the waves onto the beach during my night swim. I got up and stretched, filling my lungs with the pure sea air. I felt like a new man.

The fishermen's pirogues were already on the way back, lit up by the horizontal morning light. I took a few steps by the water's edge, my feet carving into the sand traces destined to be wiped out by the next wave in a gentle murmur of foam. Out at sea, a liner was carrying hundreds of passengers to discover the Celebes, Java, or Borneo.

I saw a little girl alone on the beach, no doubt the daughter of one of the few tourists to discover this place. She was perhaps five or six. Armed with a stick, she was carefully drawing something on the sand. She saw me come up, and, when I was next to her, she gave me a rapid smile, looking away from her drawing only for a second.

"What is it?" I asked her.

"A liner, of course," she replied in a hurt tone, carrying on drawing.

"Do you like boats?"

"Yes. I used to want to be a ship's captain."

"You've changed your mind?"

"Yes, because it's too difficult for me."

She said this with regret in her voice.

"How do you know?"

"My grandfather told me. He says it's a job for boys, not girls."

She was putting the finishing touches on her drawing, displaying a little sad look that broke my heart.

"What's your name?"

"Andy."

"Listen, Andy, look at me."

She dropped her stick and turned toward me. I knelt in the sand, putting myself at her height.

"I am sure your grandfather loves you a lot and wants what's best for you. But I'm going to tell you something. Like a secret that you'll always keep with you. Would you like that?"

"Yes."

"Andy, don't ever let anyone tell you what you're not capable of doing. It's for you to choose and live your life."

She looked me in the eyes and remained

thoughtful for a moment. Then her serious air gradually disappeared, giving way to a smile that lit up her whole face. She walked off confidently, looking out to sea, where the liner was making its way on the horizon.

ABOUT THE AUTHOR

Laurent Gounelle is a personal development specialist who trained in humanities at the University of California, Santa Cruz. Besides lecturing at Clermont-Ferrand University, he is now a consultant and takes part in international seminars. His two books have sold more than a million copies worldwide. They are based on the principles of neuro-linguistic programming (NLP).

I WON'T LEAVE WITHOUT TELLING YOU WHERE I'M GOING

LAURENT GOUNELLE

"Beneath me, 360 feet farther down, lay Paris, offering herself to me. Her twinkling lights were so many winking, calling eyes. Patiently, aware she was irresistible, she was waiting for my blood to come and fertilize her."

Looking down from the top of the Eiffel Tower, Alan Greenmor stands contemplating his life—determined to end it—when a mysterious stranger named Dubreuil convinces him to change his mind. In return, Dubreuil forges a path for Alan that will shape his destiny.

I Won't Leave Without Telling You Where I'm Going, the sensational new book by best-selling author Laurent Gounelle, explores the fragility of life and the possibilities that are presented to us in the unlikeliest circumstances.